THE FAERIE MASTER

AARON'S KISS SERIES BOOK 8

KATHI S. BARTON

This is a work of fiction. Names, characters, places, and incidents are products of the author's imagination or are used fictitiously and are not to be construed as real. Any resemblance to actual events, locations, organizations, or person, living or dead, is entirely coincidental.

World Castle Publishing
Pensacola, Florida

Copyright © Kathi S. Barton 2012
ISBN: 9781938243752
First Edition World Castle Publishing June 20, 2012
http://www.worldcastlepublishing.com

Cover: Karen Fuller
Photos: Shutterstock.com
Editor: Brieanna Robertson

CHAPTER 1

"Cade! There's a phone call for you. No personal calls while you're working. Hurry up with it too."

"Yeah, yeah. I hear you. Bite me, you jackass." She went to the phone and barked in the receiver, "Cade. What do you want?"

"I've been trying to contact you for a week. I have a job that you need to do for me and I'll pay whatever you want. But it has to be done Friday."

"Who is this?" Cade Smith knew who it was. She would recognize his voice anywhere. She just did not like him and had told him last week that she was through working for his lying, cheating ass.

"You know fucking well who this is. It's Gabriel Sheets. When can we meet to discuss the details of this takeover? Like I said, it has to be complete by Friday or neither of us gets paid."

"I'm not getting paid, not that you were ever very good about that part anyway. I don't work for you anymore, remember? Not now, not next week, not in a hundred years. I quit. Don't call me again." The phone slamming in the hook felt good to her.

Going back to the stove, she flipped the two burgers and adjusted the flame under the fried potatoes. When the meat was nearly done Cade put slices of cheese on one of them, buttered both buns, top and bottom, and slid them on the grill at the last minute. Picking up the skillet by the handle she tossed half the home fries onto each plate and scooped the burgers and buns up together. She was just putting the pickle on the plates when Paul called back again.

"Cade, the fucking phone is for you again. Tell people my number again and I'll fucking beat your ass. I got no time to be running back here to tell you it's for you."

"I didn't give them the number, fuck-tard, you did. And I told you to tell him that I wasn't coming to the phone. Besides, the walking will do you a world of good. Orders up." She stomped to the pay phone and growled. "Listen you halfwit, I quit. Q-u-i-t! You call here again and I will personally hunt you down, cut off your dick, and serve it to the rats you have as house guests. Fuck off." Taking a deep breath to continue she heard a faint "oh, my," then waited to see if whoever it was would say anything. She actually found herself hoping it was Sheets again.

"Miss Cade, it is I, Duncan. I hope I have not caught you at an inconvenient time. You did say to give you a call when I needed your assistance."

Cade closed her eyes and laid her head on the wall beside the phone. Shit, shit, and double shit. Mr. Duncan. She had met him several weeks ago at the grocery store. They had struck up a conversation about cooking and he mentioned that Miss Penny, the lady who cooked for her ladyship, was going on a much needed vacation. She told him that if he did not find a cook before she left Cade would come and help him out.

"Yeah, Duncan, it's fine. I take it you didn't find a cook to replace Penny, huh? I told you I'd help you out. When do you need me to start?"

"Oh, Miss Cade, that would be most excellent. If you could please come by tomorrow morning to make breakfast for the children before they are to be dispatched to the school that would be very helpful. I'm sorry to have put things until the very last moment, but the woman who was to come and help has decided that she would feel safer at a different location."

Safer? Whatever. Cade did not care why the other woman couldn't do it. She was just happy for the opportunity to make some extra cash. Quitting for Gabriel didn't hurt her financially; he seldom paid on time anyway if he ever did, but she did want to find a place to live with running water and heat all the time before winter.

"Just tell me where to go and I'll be there at around six in the morning. Is that too early or too late to feed the kids? And leave me a list of things they can or can't eat. I wouldn't want to poison anyone on my first day." She started to laugh, but he stopped her short.

"Oh no, Miss Cade. No, we would be most displeased with you if you tried that. I do believe his lordship would be very angry. Oh yes, very angry indeed."

"I was kidding, Duncan. I can cook very well. I'll see you at six then. And thanks for helping me out."

She went back to the kitchen and started building the orders that had come in while she had been gone. Her assistant Paula, Paul's daughter, was setting up the chips and other stuff that went with the grilled ham and cheese and the rare steak when Cade threw some par-boiled potatoes in the now clean skillet. She was thinking about the gig with the MacManuses with a smile on her face. Two weeks. Oh yeah, that would certainly help her apartment fund.

~~~

"Your ladyship, Miss Cade will be here at six to feed the children. Her references are impeccable. Also, one of her bosses said that she had a fine tushie that you could bounce quarters off of. I'm not sure how that would help with her ability to feed this household, but I did write it down for you as you asked."

Aaron picked up the pillow under his hip and tried to put it to his mouth before he hurt himself trying not to laugh. He knew that Duncan seldom got the little references and slang that people said to him and most times, it did not matter. Then there were times when he could swear that Dunc sat in the kitchen and wrote out the most ridiculous things ever just to see if anyone noticed that he had screwed it up. Looking over at his mate he realized she was having as hard a time as he was in keeping a straight face.

"Thank you, Duncan. You just never know what might or might not come in handy working in this house. I thank...I thank you for your help in this. I do hope she lasts longer than...what was her name, Aaron?"

He glared at her. She knew that in order to answer her he would have to take his pillow away from his mouth and that would hurt Duncan's feelings. So he just shrugged instead of answering.

"I believe her name was Candy Apple, my ladyship. Or was it Apple Candy? I know it had something to do with a fruit."

Aaron stuffed the pillow further into his mouth. If Duncan stayed in the room much longer he was going to have to replace the pillows again. This was the third time he had had to replace the couch because he had refused to deal with him in the kitchen and he had bitten the other pillows in half. Aaron knew there was no "dealing" with Duncan, he just was.

"Now that I think on it, I believe it was Candice Market. She did seem to be on the slight nervous side when she came here. I think we might be well rid of her."

"Ah, yes. That's it, not a fruit at all but a place to purchase it. Master, are you unwell? You look as if you may explode. I do believe we should call Master Thomas in. You may need for him to give you something for what ails you."

Aaron couldn't help it. He shimmered out of the room and to his lair. Once out of Duncan's sight and hearing he crumpled to the floor in gales of laughter. He was sure that Sara was going to be upset, but simply couldn't contain himself any longer.

"The least you could have done was wait for me. I swear to you, Aaron, that man makes this up just to see if we will laugh at him. Candy Apple—where on earth did he hear that? It sounds like a porn name."

"I was thinking the same thing. Christ, that man is something else. Hopefully Penny's temporary replacement doesn't go screaming into the night. There are days when I want to. By the way, what do we know about this girl?"

Aaron hated to bring new people into his home. It meant someone else knew the inner workings of what happened and who the key players were. But he knew that relying on Duncan to fix three meals a day for two weeks would be worth the extra trouble it might cause.

"Pete did a thorough check on her. There wasn't much that she could narrow down without her social security number. Miss Smith told Duncan that she had just moved to this area a little over a year ago. She works whenever they need her at the restaurant on Tenth Street and Paul Chrisman, her boss, said that she's the best short order cook he knows. He said that she lives over the restaurant most nights when it's chilly out. He doesn't have a clue where she stays when not there. And that was the only address she gave us besides a Post Office box. Duncan liked her. He said they spent an enjoyable afternoon at the farmers market downtown and that he had met her there a few more times on Saturdays."

"Do you think she's homeless? I hate to think of a woman out alone, especially since we've both had firsthand experience with this. Every time I think about you living in that van all those months I get chills. You were lucky, not all women are."

Aaron had met Sara at her job and when she had gotten hurt saving his life he found out she was living in her van wherever she could park it. She even took baths in a nearby stream. He held open his arms and she came and sat on his lap. He loved this woman more than anything on earth.

"Yes, all of us were. Shade too. I hope this girl works out. I know it's only for a couple of weeks, but she'll be in our home. Aaron, have you heard from Shawn yet? Wasn't he supposed to be here a few days ago?"

"Yes. I've tried contacting him and to reach out to him, but I hit a wall. I've tried a couple of others that I know he sometimes stays with and nothing. His current master is pretty bad and he told me that he'll explain when he gets here. Shawn is older than me, if you can believe that, and he's never shown any kind of inclination of becoming his own master. I'm hoping that's what he wants to talk about or that he wants to stay here. I'd welcome him."

"You welcome everyone, love. As for him being older than you, I didn't realize that things could be older than dirt. Geez, the guy must be positively decrepit."

Aaron turned Sara around into his arms when she tried to pull away from him. When he pressed her against his body he felt his need for her stir. This woman, above all others, made him feel things he'd never felt before. His need for her never ceased to amaze him. His mouth crushed against hers and he took.

Her body responded to his need immediately. He lifted her up so that her soft folds met intimately with his hard cock. As soon as Sara wrapped her legs around his hips he took them to the floor. Pulling away from her, he was on his knees between her legs on either side of him.

He rested back on his heels while he looked down at her. "Take off your blouse, Sara. I need you. I want to fuck you right now."

While she pulled her blouse from her jeans and unbuttoned it he worked at the snap and zipper of her pants. Standing to pull them off her, he stripped off his own shirt and tossed it behind him. The sight of her in only her bra and panties made his cock jerk hard in his pants.

"Take off your bra. Make your nipples hard for me, baby. Make them ache for me." He felt his fangs drop in anticipation of tasting her. He loved her taste, her scent that she exuded just for him. When his eyes began to turn, her body was outlined in a deep red that made his need sharp. Stripping his pants off with his boxer briefs, he stood before her naked and stroked his cock while she watched, her nipples beading hard as she rolled and squeezed them for him.

"Aaron, please. I need you. I want to feel you inside of me. I want you to drink from me. Make me come hard. Please, baby. I want to feel you come deep inside of me."

Aaron knew he wouldn't last if she touched him now. He needed to take the edge off, needed to sip from her so that he would last longer than it would take for him to enter her. Dropping back down, he ran his hands up her thighs and his fingers under her tiny thong. Gripping it in his hands, he looked into her eyes and he tore it from her body. Her cry of hunger made his fangs burst more through his gums.

"It'll have to be hard, Sara. Fast, hard, and dirty. Roll over for me. I need you too much to do this any other way."

When she rolled to her belly and curved her body up over her knees he growled at her. Her arousal was strong and he could see her pussy was wet. Pushing her head down to the floor he nudged his cock at her entrance. She coated him with her juices. Grabbing her hips and pulling her back against him he slammed into her hard and deep. Her answering groan nearly sent him over the edge. Pulling out to nearly the tip and slamming again he felt her grip around him; her tight sheath wrapped around him and sucked him deeper. He felt his climax grip his balls and the tingle of it run up his spine. Reaching his hand around her front and finding her clit he pulled hard on it then squeezed. Over and over he tormented it until she started to grip him tighter.

"Aaron, now! Please, I'm coming now. Bite me."

Leaning forward, he licked at her shoulder and then sank his fangs deep into her. The hot, spicy blood filled his mouth as she came, milking him and bringing him over the edge with her. As he filled her with his seed she fed him, nourished him. Sealing the tiny prick marks with his tongue, he pulled her up so that both of them were on their knees and he was still buried deep inside of her. Aaron pressed his wrist to her mouth and moved slowly inside of her again as she bit into him and drank, bringing her to another climax. As soon as she sealed the wound with her saliva he tilted her back and took her throat.

Taking enough to sustain him, he licked her throat and kissed the tiny wound. He held her to his body, feeling her heartbeat return to normal and her breathing slow. He wanted her again, but not now. He would move them to the bed soon.

"Aaron, I love you very much. I don't know what I would have done without you and our children all these years. You've made me so very happy."

"And you me, my love. You have given me reason to live and reason to rise. Let's get to bed so that I can make love to you properly."

Lifting her gently in his arms he carried her to the bed and snuggled in behind her. Holding her to his body he felt when she relaxed against him. Smiling, he was warmed by her security of being next to him. Reaching out again and hitting the same wall he hoped that Shawn was all right. Safe and secure wherever he was as well.

CHAPTER 2

Cade was at the MacManus house at five-thirty the next morning. Duncan let her in the back door and smiled at her bike. She did not have any other mode of transportation right now so it was either ride in the rain or walk in it. Riding seemed dryer.

"You must be soaked through, miss. Let me retrieve a towel from the laundry room and we will get you dry posthaste. You may remove your shoes if you would like. They will dry nicely in the mud room."

She loved the way he talked, so prim and proper. She thought that he sounded like he was very old, but did not look much older than maybe forty. While he was getting a towel she took off her boots and put them upside down on the rug. The left one had a huge hole in the bottom and let water in like it was its job. She had put the need for shoes lower on the list of things she needed two weeks ago when she needed to buy tampons. Go figure.

"This is a great kitchen, Duncan. I bet you could cook for an army in here if you needed to. When will the kids come in?" The noise of the swinging door was all the warning she got.

Two of the most gorgeous kids she had ever seen came busting in. There was no doubt that they were related. They looked so opposite to each other that Cade knew they favored a parent each. Must be really pretty people.

"Are you the new cook? I would like pancakes and bacon, please, but I don't like eggs. Do you know what they are?" the little boy said as he pulled out a stool to sit on.

"Yeah, I know. I can cook most anything and with a recipe I can cook that too. I can make you pancakes this morning if you want, but I had planned on something different. It's your choice."

Duncan had told her that she could cook them whatever they wanted for breakfast—short of something too sweet. No one had any food allergies that he knew of and yes, she could bring her own skillet. Cade loved her cast iron skillet.

"I like waffles. Pancakes are just soggy bread with syrup on them. And I don't care for sausage unless it's in links. You can make those for me."

Before Duncan could step in Cade looked at the little prima donna. "Nope, today we have pancakes and bacon. He spoke politely and without the attitude. Drop it if you want something special. I want to be treated like a person not a servant. Deal?" She stood there for a few minutes before Cade realized she was searching her mind. She let her until she started to dip deeper, then pushed back with a warning. "Don't tread were you aren't invited, little girl. I've more control and I've been doing this longer." When Lizzy staggered back Cade winked at her.

"I've been practicing for weeks on being gentle. How did you know I was there? I can do everyone else's without them knowing it." All she needed to do to make it complete, Cade thought, was to stomp her foot.

"Maybe they didn't care that you were there. I do. Stay out or I push back. I'm not going to tell you again. I don't need this gig badly enough to have you trampling in my mind."

"Elizabeth MacManus, I believe that we've had this conversation before. You'll apologize to Miss Smith right now. And you're grounded. No computer for a week."

"Mr. MacManus, please don't do that. We are just setting up our boundaries here. She should know the people around her and I'm a stranger to her. But she got her information and then dug deeper. I was just explaining that she went too far. I pick my battles and this one isn't worth her disliking me for the few weeks I'll be here."

The man looked ready to say more, but the woman walking into the room took everyone's attention. Now Cade could see that she had been right, each child did indeed take after a parent. Mrs. MacManus, however, looked ready to do battle.

"Elizabeth, I believe your father told you to apologize to Miss. Smith. Miss Smith, in the future, if you have a problem with one of my children please let me know. I don't want any trouble with them."

Cade did not know what she expected, but this had not been it. She fully expected to be sent packing and was surprised and pleased to be able to keep her job. She would bet real money that Elizabeth had a terrible habit of mind raping whenever it suited her.

Cade was also surprised to find another telepath, especially one as strong as the child. She turned to the refrigerator to hide her surprise at the turn of events. Pulling out the items to cook what the boy wanted she gently reached out and made her own discoveries. Vampires. Holy flipping shit! She turned sharply to Mr. MacManus. She knew she looked shocked.

"I won't harm you. You can believe me. I don't know how much you know about our kind, but once mated we never feed from others unless it's a dire emergency. If you'd like to leave I'll understand, but you'll not remember us or what you know if you do."

"But I'll leave intact? I didn't...no one...fuck!" The children laughed as Cade flushed. "Sorry. I'm just not...you really are? But its daylight—I'm sorry, you must think I'm stupid."

"No. On the contrary, I think you've shown great strength in not running out the door. If you have questions now or in the next two weeks please ask them. I swear to you you'll leave every day with the amount of blood you came here with. I can stand the sun this early because I'm very old."

"Yeah, he's old all right. But he's telling you the truth, Miss Smith, we won't harm you. Not without provocation." Sara was pulling out a glass to pour herself and the children some juice as she spoke.

"Yeah, okay. It's Cade, and so when I leave here today you'll what...erase my memories? I'll have to meet you new every day? Have we met already?"

"No, this is your first day. And no, as long as you give me your word we'll leave your memories intact. But for now I have business to attend to, then I must retire." With a kiss to his kids and a hug to his...mate, he started to leave.

Walking to the stove where Cade was, it took everything she had not to cringe when he stepped close to her. When he put out his hand to her it took her a second to realize he was asking for the promise. She was proud that her hand did not shake.

"I won't tell anyone. Not that I believe it myself, but I won't tell anyone. Just, you know, keep your teeth in your mouth and not at any part of my body if you don't mind."

He was still laughing when the door stopped swinging behind him as he left the room, really fucking fast. Cade looked over at Mrs. MacManus. "And you don't need to, you know, leave either?" Again she was proud of herself, no tremor in her voice.

"No. I will have some pancakes and bacon this morning. Thank you."

The rest of the morning was a blur of activities. The kids ate like they had been starved for a week. Duncan showed her how to find things in the pantry—it was organized like a back room at most restaurants she worked at—and where to find the spices and other pots and pans in the oversized room. When the kitchen was cleaned up, she asked to help out around the house and Duncan asked if she could please help with the laundry.

"The machine gives me fits, Miss Cade. I cannot seem to make it function properly. Just the other day I put in white laundry and it came out a very odd color. I believe it has a curse on it. Miss Penny could seem to persuade it to do whatever she needed. Maybe it prefers the gentle touch of a pretty woman."

"Duncan, you're a charmer. I'll be happy to do the clothes. Just show me where the washer is and I'll be set. I have another shirt in my bag, do you think anyone would mind if I put this one in the dryer?"

"Oh no, miss, you may use it. Please be advised, though, that it does tend to make things smaller on occasion. I've had to replace many of her ladyship's lovely sweaters because of it."

After assuring him that she would be careful Cade changed her shirt and threw the wet one in the dryer. While it dried she started separating the laundry and setting up the loads. She did not mind the laundry; it gave her something to do. At two she was fixing dinner when a man and woman just opened the door and came in behind her.

"Son of a bitch! Don't do that! Crap. Is it going to be like this for the entire two weeks, people popping in and out like jack in the boxes?" Cade held her hand over her chest as she glared at the couple.

"Usually someone knows we're about to 'pop' in, but I see that Duncan isn't about. Do you know where Sara is? She and I are...are those apple dumplings? Can I have one?" Without waiting for Cade to answer the woman scooped one up and put it on a plate. Cade reached into the freezer and handed her the ice cream.

"And you are?" Amazingly, the man sat and scooped one up for himself as well. Cade thought they were rude, but then she did not know this household. Maybe this was the norm.

"Alastriona Wolfe and this is my mate, Bradley. He's the alpha. I take it you know what we all are since you work for the master."

Cade didn't know what to say to that. She knew Mr. MacManus was a vamp and that Sara was something close. Not a clue what Duncan was or the kids. It took her a few seconds to figure out what these two were.

"Dogs? I don't...you're dogs of some kind? I think I'm—no, I'm pretty sure I've lost my mind. Next thing there'll be dragons and fairies coming around."

"Oh no, the dragon stays in the otherworld—too many people around for him. There are some nymphs and fairies, but they don't show up until later, vampires you know. But we're not dogs. Bradley is the alpha for the Brotherhood of Gray wolf pack. I'm his bitch. And you would be?"

"Well, of course you are. Why not? I'm Cade Smith." Cade sat in the chair hard and when the dryer made a noise signaling that it had finished its cycle she went to the laundry room. She hoped they would be gone before she returned. The woman was, the man was not.

"I think you might be a tad overwhelmed. We didn't know that Dunc had found someone to replace the one who chickened out at the last minute. How much do you know about the people you work for?"

He didn't trust her and for some reason that hurt her. She only wanted to make some extra cash so she wouldn't have to live in the cave again this winter. She turned her back to him and started to braise the pork chops in her skillet.

"To answer your question, yes, but 'tad' doesn't even come close. As for the MacManuses, I'm temporary, and

Mr. MacManus claims I'll be safe here. That's all I want to know at this point. I want no trouble from them or you. I need the extra money and that's all."

"Miss Smith, I'm—"

"If you'll excuse me, Mr. Wolfe, I need to be anywhere but in this kitchen with you right now. I do hope you'll be not here when I return. I'm sorry, but as you have pointed out, I've had a lot thrown at me today." Cade went back to the laundry room. She bent to take the clothes out of the dryer when she heard him finally leave the kitchen. It was then that she let the tears fall. She felt stupid; she never cried. But not having someone trust her was something she hated more than anything.

Coming out after folding the towels she took the pork chops out of the skillet and put them on a platter. The chopped onions went in one of the kitchen pans next with some thyme. When the onions were browned she put the chops back in the skillet with some peeled potatoes and carrots. After putting the lid on and slipping it in the oven, she turned the temperature down to three hundred degrees and set the timer. She was just drying her own skillet when Mrs. MacManus walked in.

"Everything is ready. There are rolls in the bread drawer in the bag and I've put out some fresh butter to serve with them. When the timer goes off just pull out the pan and serve. I'll clean up in the morning if Duncan will leave it."

"Cade, Bradley said that you and he might have—"

"Mrs. MacManus, I'll tell you what I told him, I'm temporary. I don't care what you guys do as long as no one has me for dinner. I need the money more than I care to admit, but I'm not a quitter. I'll be here tomorrow."

"All right, but he would like to explain what he meant. Bradley is a good man. He would never do anything to upset you. He wants to know if you'll talk to him."

"I have another job to go to. Tell Mr. Wolfe everything is fine. I'm sure he's a very wonderful person. Good night." Cade went out into the mud room and quickly slipped on her boots. They were semi-dry and she laced them quickly. The rain had slowed, but it was still coming down and after three tries her bike started. She was at the outer gate when she realized she forgot her other shirt on the dryer. Oh well, might need it tomorrow. The rain looks really dug in.

CHAPTER 3

Shawn MacFarland wandered around the woods most of the night. He couldn't seem to get his bearings on where he was. Sitting down next to a tree he closed his eyes against the pain and took deep breaths. He needed to feed, and soon. He couldn't remember what had happened after he had come out of the bar in Columbus, but he was bleeding badly.

Looking down at the wound he tried again to piece together what had happened. The woman he had been with was coming out to have sex with him and to let him feed. The latter she wouldn't remember, but she would let him. She had seemed tense as soon as they walked out onto the sidewalk and then...nothing. He woke up in the woods with blood on his clothes and the knife, a switchblade, still stuck in his ribs.

Whatever it had been it had not been robbery. His wallet with his credit cards and money had been still in his pocket. His car keys too. He just couldn't seem to remember the name of the bar, how he had gotten here. But worst of all he only knew his name because of his driver's license and nothing more about himself.

Oh, he knew he was a vampire, that he had been one since the mid-third century. He knew that he had powers and other than being able to move quickly couldn't remember what they were or how to use them. The name of a friend was just there, but he couldn't remember it either. There was something else too, something just beyond his reach that he should know, but that too eluded him. Getting up, he started walking until he came to a deep cave.

~~~

"I'd feel better if you stayed here tonight, Cade. The weather is supposed to turn wicked and all you need is to catch pneumonia. No one sleeps up there and you'll be warm."

She wanted to, and after a few minutes of doing the pros and cons of whether or not to stay, she told Paul she would. "But only if I close up. That way Mary Margaret will be grateful to me and I'll get some brownie points. And you, my friend, might get laid. The entire bar would be happy if you would get some more often. You're a real bastard when you're horny."

Cade grinned when he looked shocked. Then he gave her a smile that looked less friendly and more predatory. It made her think of the people she had met today. A quick shiver when down her spine. Vampires and wolves, oh my.

"Deal. Its Mary Margaret's birthday tomorrow anyway. This will put me in good with her too. And you aren't allowed to comment on my sex life until you have one of you own. You haven't been out on a date in all the time you've lived around here. What, the men around here not good enough for you?"

Cade just smiled. It wasn't that, but she was not going to tell him she was too tired to try and figure most men out. She liked men, enjoyed them even. It was just who had time to get to know anyone when one was working four jobs and trying to save every penny made? Not her.

When the kitchen closed down at midnight she went out to the bar to finish up and tend bar. Paul left sometime after twelve-thirty. At one-forty-five she called last call and then at two-ten closed up the bar. By the time she had cleaned up the last of the glasses and swept behind the bar it was nearly four. Wondering if she could get an hour in before having to leave for the MacManus' Cade decided to take a long, hot bath and shave her legs.

At five, with the rain still coming down, she went out to her bike and tried to get it going. After several tires and getting soaked to her skin Cade called a cab. She hated to do it. Not only would it cost her to get to the MacManus', she would have to pay to get back here again too. By the time the taxi showed up she had changed again and had bundled her clothes in a bag, hoping that she could throw them in the dryer when she got to work.

At six-thirty she had the batter made up for waffles and the dishes from the night before put away. Duncan told her that he could load the dishwasher without any problems so he would make sure they were done.

"Miss, I was wondering if you had anything from the grocery store that you needed? Her ladyship and I are going into town this morning when the young ones are off to school. I could pick up whatever you needed."

A thousand and one things entered her head. Everything from a bag of really good potato chips to a newer car. Shampoo that cost more than seventy-nine cents on clearance, tuna that came fresh and not from a can, a bra that lasted more than three months, shoes without holes, the list was endless and unfortunately not what he meant.

"Thank you, Duncan, but I don't know what the people here eat. You'd be a better judge of that than me. I'll cook whatever they want me to."

Lizzy came into kitchen first. She really was a pretty little girl, Cade thought. She had made the little girl the requested waffles and sausage links and Lizzy thanked her politely. When Mac came in a few minutes later he was upset about something and Mrs. MacManus was too.

"You'd better drop the attitude, young man. I'll not have you acting like you have no idea why you're being punished. If you don't make the grade today then you won't go to Brent's birthday party. That's final." Sara growled slightly in the back of her throat when he glared at her as his mother left the room.

"He has a math test today and he thinks math is stupid. Mom told him that if he didn't make at least a C then he couldn't go to our cousin's birthday party. He'll be nine on Saturday. He has the best parties," Lizzy explained as she poured syrup on her waffle.

"Mac, what is it about math that you don't like? It's the best thing in the world and used for everything. There isn't one thing in the world that math doesn't have some kind of effect on."

"Yeah, right. Mom told you to say that, didn't she? I hate it. I mean, who cares how many teaspoons are in a cup or stuff? I don't."

"There are forty-eight. And you should care. Math is the only way to keep things moving in the world. Without it there would be chaos and nothing would work. Without math there could be no time, no television, and no cars. Math is the universal standard; math is what holds everything together."

Cade pulled out a bowl and then the flour, eggs, and baking powder. She set them in front of Mac. Then she did the same for Lizzy. "Here, you both are going to make the waffle batter. Lizzy will use the measuring spoons and cups, you won't. Which do you think will taste better?"

She helped them both, giving Lizzy a short lesson in how to measure, and watched as Mac tried to measure the ingredients in the bowl in the same amounts as his sister. When they were finished she cooked them both and put them on the plate. It was obvious which was going to taste better.

"Okay, so you have to have math to cook, but what else? I don't use it for nothing. I still hate it."

"You don't use it for anything, and you do. How does your mother pick out your clothes? Does she just go to the store and grab stuff for you? No, she needs sizes. It would be ridiculous to think you and your father were the same size. What about your body? Did you know that you are made up of all sorts of math equations? If you didn't have enough fluids in you you'd be dehydrated. If you're dehydrated then you get constipated. Without enough food, the right amounts of each kind of food, you'd die, right?"

"My dad doesn't eat food and he does just fine. What about that?"

Okay that threw her, but she would deal with that later. "Your mom, she...she is the...you know, I'm not going there. But if your dad didn't get the right amount of...of, shit, of blood then he'd die. He has to have a measured amount or he is a dead man. Same principle with everything. I'll tell you what, you work on it all day and when I come in tomorrow, if you can think up one thing that has nothing to do with math then I'll make you my famous pizza. I make the greatest too. What do you say?"

"What about my test today? Mom said I have to make a C or I'm in trouble. I don't want to."

"Ah, so you can make a C, but you choose not to. Stupid thing to do, don't you think? Bring your mom down on your head because you think you're smarter than she is? Nah, not touching that one. But I will tell you, if you can make better than a B I'll give you five bucks—ten if you make an A."

"Hey, that's not fair. How can I make ten bucks? I want money too," Lizzy said with a pout.

Cade looked at the two of them. They lived in a house worth more than she would see in five lifetimes and she was paying them money to make good grades. Shaking her head she thought it over.

"Okay, Lizzy. Let's see. You're a smart girl, so we'll make yours different. You have to be nice and polite to three people today, not once be snarky or anything, and I'll give you ten bucks. If you are nasty to one—just one, you have to...you have to do dishes after dinner tonight. And without complaint."

Cade was sure the girl could do it, even more sure that Mac could make the grade. Her concern was what the parents would say when they found out. Neither kid said anything when Sara came back into the kitchen. And Sara did not say anything when Cade started cleaning up the waffle disaster.

The morning was quiet after the kids, Sara, and Duncan left. Mr. MacManus came in shortly before they left and had left the kitchen when everyone else did. He didn't say much; he seemed upset and distracted. Cade put her things in the dryer after gaining permission from Duncan again and set about making lasagna for dinner.

The pantry had bottled sauce, but Cade liked to make her own so, taking the cans of tomatoes and other sauces she would need into the kitchen, she made a huge pot of rich basil sauce. She hesitated about the garlic and then decided to not add it in. She had no idea what it would do to anyone and figured on not taking the chance. The homemade noodles where tricky in that she had only a rolling pin to roll them out, but she got them at the right thickness after rolling for an hour. Stacking the noodles and sauce pattern in the pan, she put it on the counter with a note on how to cook it. Buttered bread slices where also set out on a sheet tray with written instructions on how to cook them as well. By three she had cleaned up her mess and was waiting on the taxi at the end of the drive.

By the time she was being dropped off at the bar again the rain had stopped. But she was soaked again and was glad for the dry clothes she had with her. Changing in the bathroom she rolled her wet things up and put them in the bag again. If this kept up she was going to owe the MacManuses for the extra electric. Going into the warm kitchen she started working. At around nine she started feeling crappy. By midnight she knew she was sick.

When the bar closed at two-thirty Cade walked out into the chilly spring night and shivered. Her bike started on the first try and she could have cried. Paul drove off when he was sure she was going to be able to drive home and then so did Don. Pulling to the end of the parking lot she went left instead of right. She'd told Paul she was going to her new apartment, but went to the caves instead.

She had come across the caves her second week in living out of doors. They were quiet and she loved the feeling of being deep inside of them. There was a natural spring in the one she stayed in the most and when she had gone deeper into it she had discovered the most beautiful drawings on the walls. She knew a discovery like this should be reported, but the thought of sharing such a find, her find, just did not set well with her. No one knew about it but her and the occasional animal that wandered in during the winter months. After seeing to her bike she walked the last half mile in. It was nearly three-thirty when she finally lay down.

The lack of sound woke her. Nothingness surrounded her. Opening her eyes to the deep darkness she thought she heard a faint sound and, before she could ask who was there, a hand was over her mouth and a heavy body over her. She couldn't move. Terror gripped her hard.

"Don't say a word. I'm not going to hurt you. I'm hungry and I need you. If you allow me to feed from you I'll make it good for you. I'm too weak to take your memory, but I will make you enjoy it."

Cade screamed behind his hand as he nuzzled her neck. Fear made her body drench in sweat and her heart pound in her chest. She reached out to him.

"Please, don't. I don't want this. You can't do this, I beg you."

"I'm sorry. I've no choice. I've been without food for weeks and I need to survive. I wish I could take this memory away, but I'm too weak and it's nearly sunrise."

When his tongue traced over the vein in her throat she felt the first stir of need curl in her belly. When the man pulled back and looked down at her she thought he was going to stop. She could feel him pressed between her legs, his thigh hard against her mound.

"I want your throat, but if you'd prefer, I can take your wrist. I'm going to feed from you either way, but I'll give you the choice."

"Please don't do this. Please let me go," Cade begged behind his hand. When he shook his head and lowered to her neck she screamed at him, "Wrist!"

"Pity. I would love to feel your hot pulse in my mouth as I drink from you. You smell like home to me, warm bread and apples. Fresh grass and sunshine. I am truly sorry for this."

Taking her hand to his mouth he looked deep into her eyes as she watched his fangs lengthen and stretch from his gums. She turned away from him when he opened his mouth to show the gleam of them. With the hand over her mouth he turned her head toward his and she looked into his deep red eyes.

The pain of him biting her jerked through her body and when he drew his first mouthful she heard him groan. She felt his cock harden and lengthen against her belly. When he moved against her, shifting so that his cock was between her legs, tight against her apex, he rocked into her. Cade's breath caught. As he drank from her he rocked against her until she thought she would scream. She didn't even notice when he took his hand from her mouth or when he wrapped it over her breast and tweaked her nipple hard. Soon she was wrapping her legs around his hips as he continued to drink, continued to rock into her.

"That's it, baby. Feel me. Feel me hard against your hot pussy. Christ, I need to bury my cock into you."

The man sat up quickly and pulled off her pants, jerking and pulling at them until she was bare beneath him. There was not a single thought in her mind to stop him, her body on fire for his. She could feel her wetness running down the crack of her ass as he stood and took off his own clothing. She could see his cock was hard and straining. The little moonlight that filtered in the mouth of the cave was enough to see that much of him. When he dropped onto her again, his engorged cock now pressing against her clit and making her soak the ground beneath her, she wrapped her legs around him again.

Cade screamed out when he entered her hard and fast. This time when he nuzzled her throat she tilted her head to allow him access. His mouth closed over her pulse and when he bit her she came apart. Her release was explosive and quick and when he slammed into her once, twice, three times more, pulling his mouth away with a swipe of his tongue, he threw back his head and poured himself into her with a roar. The last thing she remembered was him dropping back onto her body before blackness claimed her.

CHAPTER 4

Cade woke suddenly. The quietness of the cave from before was now over. She could hear the birds and other animals starting to rise for the day. Looking at her watch she realized it was nearly five. Sitting up quickly made her dizzy and she had to lie back down. After a minute of waiting for the walls to stop spinning she tried again. That's when she noticed her wrist. It had been bitten. Bitten and was still bleeding. The memory of what happened last night came rushing back at her with sudden clarity. She'd been raped, raped by a vampire.

As she made her way to the little pond she blushed with the knowledge that he had not raped her; she had been a willing participant in the entire thing. He had told her he could make it better for her; she just hadn't known that he had meant it would be better for him too. Sliding into the water she realized she was sore, sore in places she'd never been before. She supposed good sex could do that to a person and she blushed again.

By the time she was dressed in her dry clothes she had convinced herself that other than the mark on her wrist and her sore body she was fine. Walking to her bike she had convinced herself that she had been lucky and that he could have killed her if he had wanted, but for whatever reason he had not. By the time she got to the MacManus home she decided to stay in the bar from now on and to never mention this to anyone. It did not take them long to figure out what she was trying to hide.

"Miss, are you unwell? You look pale and, if you don't mind me saying so, you seem a little off skittles."

"Skittles? I'm sorry, Duncan, I don't know what you mean. I'm fine though. Just didn't sleep well last night. I'll be fine soon."

She hoped so anyway. The padding that she had put around her wrist to stop the flow of blood was already soaked through and her head was feeling decidedly fuzzy. She had to stop twice now to remember what she was doing in the middle of making cinnamon rolls for the kids. When the kids came in a few minutes later she noticed Duncan slip out with a worried look and then forgot about him when Mac showed her his math test.

"I got an A. The teacher said it was the best work I ever did. I told her that it was easy, math was in...are you all right, Cade? You look funny." He sounded so far away that she blinked several times to make sure he was still in the room with her.

"Yes. I'm good. I guess I owe you ten bucks, kiddo! Congratulations. I bet your mom was really proud of you. How about you, Lizzy? Do you get your money too?" Grabbing the counter, she hung on until she thought she could let go. She really needed to sit down.

"I don't think you're at all well. I can smell blood on you and something else. I'm getting my daddy. He'll know what to do," Mac said as he backed out of the room

Cade hoped so. But she had a feeling that it was too late for him to help her right now. The room was pitching and tossing her as if she was in a bad storm and she was without a rudder. This time when she reached for the counter it simply wasn't there. When the floor rushed up to meet her she actually welcomed it. Perhaps it would make things settle if she were lying down. That was the last thing she remembered for awhile.

~~~

Shawn came awake suddenly. The girl, the woman from this morning, was in trouble. He had taken her blood and now she was in trouble. Sitting up in the deepest part of the cave he reached for her and hit a wall. Pressing harder, he was just able to touch her when the connection was broken. Pulling the shadows around himself, he was on his way to her before he realized that he had used some of his powers that up until that moment he did not know how to use. Moving faster toward her he sensed others of his kind near her and hurried more. He reached her just as a large vamp was laying her on a bed. Crashing through the window he let go of his humanity and the shadows instantly.

He hit the man with all his might, knocking the man across the room and into the wall beyond. Shawn's fangs lengthened and stretched, his need to protect the girl from the man imminent. The force of his fist hitting the man again threw him through the wall and into the next room. Stalking to him again Shawn froze in mid-step and fell forward onto the carpeted floor.

"Christ, what the fuck happened? Sara, are you all right? Who was...Shawn? What are you doing?"

He couldn't move, but he could see the man. A faint memory touched his mind, but he couldn't hold onto it long enough to make sense of it. He strained to stand and...he was not sure what he would do, but he did not like being held like this. Magic of some sort.

"I've got him in a hold. He won't be able to move. But he's strong. This is your friend? Why is he trying to kill you?"

The woman looked down at him then at the woman on the bed. He growled at her. He wasn't sure why it was important to make them stay away from the woman, but he knew that he would kill anyone who tried to touch her again.

The man he'd been trying to kill kneeled down in front of him. Again, his mind tried to grab something, but like before, it was gone. He stared at the man trying to remember, trying to pull something out.

"Shawn, do you know who I am? It's Aaron, Aaron MacManus. We've been friends for centuries. You were supposed to be here days ago, almost two weeks now. I don't know what happened, I couldn't reach you." He started to reach forward when Shawn growled again. "I'm going to touch your head. I want to see if you're hurt, don't fight me. Sara, my mate, has you in a hold that you won't be able to break."

The calm of his voice moved over him. For as much as he wanted to fight against his touch he was comforted with his voice, or the memory of it. He closed his eyes at the overwhelming need to pull him into an embrace.

"Aaron, Cade has been hurt, almost drained by someone. And she smells like him. Do you think he bit her and took too much? Oh, Christ, look! He didn't seal this off. She's bleeding to death."

The man disappeared from his view then he was standing over the girl. Shawn growled again, this time deeper and with more meaning. He was going to kill this man when he was let go. She was his, his...his something. Food, she was his food. But he knew that wasn't right either.

The man who called himself Aaron came back and Shawn tried to lunge at him. Need to protect was beating at him and he didn't understand. Pain radiated from his head, not like it had when he had first woke up, but almost as intense. He realized the man, Aaron he had called himself, was talking.

"...dies. You understand me, Shawn. You fed from her and she's still bleeding. You have to seal the wound or she dies. I'm going to have Sara release you, but if you try to hurt me or my mate then she'll pull you under again. The girl on the bed needs you. If you don't seal the wound you opened then I won't have any choice but to claim her as my child and turn her. I know you can understand me. If you want to help her, blink twice at me. If you don't care then come at me. Sara, release him."

"Aaron, I don't think this is a good—"

"Sara, honey, I think Cade is his mate. I don't know why he didn't seal the wounds and frankly, I don't care. But we will have to convert her if he doesn't help her. There is a huge bump at the back of his head and I'm betting that he had lost a great deal of blood if the stain on his shirt is any indication. I don't think he knows who I am either. Please, let him go. But be ready."

He tried to think, but the pain was nearly too much. The girl's need too, it was making him ache to be with her. He wanted to touch her. Blinking twice, he stared up at the man.

He could feel the hold lessen. He didn't move until he felt the bond completely gone. He sat up on the floor and looked at Aaron. His head hurt, but he could also feel the pull of the girl.

"I don't know who I am. I don't know who you are either. Something happened, I...someone stabbed me and I found her. She fed me and I took her. Tell me...tell me how to help her."

"You didn't seal the wounds on her wrist. I can feel the mark on her neck, but it's sealed. It's your mark on her. Shawn, you have to seal the one on her wrist then feed her. If you don't she will die. Do you know what she is to you?"

"You said mate. That sounds right. The word sounds right to me. You know me? We are...we're friends?"

"Yes, very good friends. I have a place you can stay. You can stay in one of the suites below ground until tonight when we can talk. It's getting late and I must retire soon, as will you. Heal her and then I'll show you to your rooms."

"She comes with me. The girl, she...I need her to be with me. I won't harm her. I just need to know that she's close, that I can touch her." He didn't know why, but he felt that if he didn't have her close enough to touch he would go insane.

"Yes, of course. As soon as you've fed her and sealed the wound you can bring her. Her name is Cade. Cade Smith. She works for my family. We'll talk more later. Sara and I will be downstairs. Come down when you're ready. But please don't linger, it's nearly noon now."

Aaron and Sara walked out. Shawn could tell Sara did not want to leave him with Cade. Hell, he wasn't sure if she should or not, but he also knew he couldn't hurt her. Getting up, he walked over to the bed and arranged her more comfortably on the blanket then looked at her.

She was beautiful. Her hair tumbled over the pillow and blanket beneath her, a red so deep it defied nature. He knew it was natural. He couldn't smell any dyes or bleaches on her. Her brows were arched perfectly over closed eyes that he remembered to be a dark blue. There were dark circles under them and her skin so pale he knew that the freckles that danced over her nose and forehead would be there to see when she was healthy and awake. Her nose was cute, though he did not know where that word had come from. It was slopped and small, a button on her face. Cheek bones stood out prominently, making him think of the queens and princesses he had met in his lifetime. Her lips were pale too, but looked plump. It was then that he realized he had not kissed her. He had taken her, came deep inside of her, but had not tasted her. Leaning close to her he could smell her blood and, with a quick brush of his mouth over hers, he picked up her bloodied wrist.

He had bitten her badly. And if he did not have the power to seal the wound he had made she would have a deep and ugly scar. Bringing her wrist to his mouth he couldn't help but taste her once more. Her spice, her flavor, surged through him. Licking his tongue over the open wound and taking a little more into his mouth, he sealed the tear in her skin.

Need rippled through him and his cock hardened more. He wanted her, all of her. But he knew that she needed his blood to live. Her heart rate was slowing, her breaths low and slow. He opened a vein on his own wrist and pressed it to her mouth. His fangs lengthened again at the thought of her drinking from him, of her sucking his blood from his vein. When she did not respond at first Shawn leaned down to her ear and spoke gently to her.

"Cade, I need you to sip from me. Drink what I offer you so that I can take to you properly this time. You've no idea how the feel of you wrapped around me felt, the way you tightened that hot pussy around my cock when you came. When we make love next time I will suckle at these hard nipples, pull them deep into my mouth and drink from them. Cade, my cock aches for you. Drink, Cade. Please, sweetheart, drink from me."

The first time her tongue touched his skin he thought he would come up off the bed. When he felt her pull on his vein he shifted around on her and, using his free hand, cupped her sex. With every pull of her mouth he pressed hard against her clit. Her moans had him leaning down and taking her cloth-covered breast into his mouth as he continued to fuck her with his fingers and hand.

"That's it, baby, drink. I need to mark you again, love. I want you to come and, when you do, I'm going to bite you and bring you to peak again. Ride my hand,

Cade. That's it, baby. Fuck, I want you. I want to tear off your clothes and slam into you. Come, Cade. Now!"

Her climax was quick. When she tightened her thighs around his hand he pulled his wrist from her mouth and, with a quick swipe of his tongue, sealed it. Then he slanted his mouth over hers as she began to scream her release. His mouth devoured her, claimed her. His tongue swept through her mouth and touched every dark, sweet place it could reach. Her hands wrapped into his hair and she pulled him close, closer still as she continued to jerk under his hand. Pulling away, working his mouth down her slender neck, he found her pulse and licked the area then plunged his fangs in quickly. A second climax as powerful as the first gripped her.

He couldn't take much, but he did feel her essence as it filled him. Only drawing enough to taste and not feed he sealed those tiny pricks as well, careful to make sure he had sealed the wound fully. As she lay there jerking and beginning to calm he nuzzled at her neck and inhaled. Warmth, apples and bread, and home. She smelled like home to him.

When he was sure she would be all right he picked her up in his arms and carried her downstairs. She was tall, he realized, and slender. Hugging her tighter to him he followed Aaron to the sublevels and laid Cade on the big bed. After Aaron left him Shawn went to strip her clothing from her. He stopped when he got to her bra and panties. He somehow knew that if she woke up naked with him in the bed next to her she would be angry. That made him smile. He was sure that she would be spectacular when she was pissed off.

CHAPTER 5

Cade woke to a dark room. The bed beneath her made her aware she was not in her cave but in a household. The last thing she remembered was the kitchen and kids. Shifting to move off the bed something tightened around her waist. Fear washed over her. A man was beside her.

Lifting the heavy arm up off her seemed simple enough, but he—and it could only be a man because of the massive size of the arm—kept pulling her back to him. She finally managed to get out from beneath him only to discover she was nearly naked. Sitting on the floor, she crawled around until she found a chair leg. Patting the seat she found a pair of pants and a shirt, but from the size she guessed they were his. Pulling on the shirt she crawled to what she hoped was the door, feeling around for her clothes as she went. And of course, when she got to the door, it was locked. She was just trying to get it opened when a click and a light flared behind her.

"It's locked. Aaron said that I was the only one able to open it once I set the lock. How are you feeling?"

"Open this. I want out now. And where are my clothes?" She looked at the man on the bed who now sat up with his back against the headboard, his chest bare.

"No. I asked you how you're feeling. You didn't answer. You look good. Delicious, as a matter of fact. Come back to bed with me." He actually patted the space beside him. She turned her back on him and tried the door again.

She heard him move. The air changed and she knew he was just behind her. A small whimper escaped her mouth before she could stop it. Pressing herself against the door to keep him from touching her she knew she was trapped. "Let me go. You have no right to keep me prisoner here. I have to go to work tonight. I have to go to work tonight and you are keeping me from it."

"You won't be working anymore. I will take care of you now. Come back to bed with me, Cade. I want to make love to you. I need you."

She pressed harder to the door. "Please? I don't want to be here. I...want this door open before I have to hurt you. I don't know who you are, I don't even want to know, just let me out of here."

She felt him step back, not far, but enough that she knew if she wanted she could let go of the door pressing deep in her belly. But she stayed where she was, not looking at him. Before he could speak she realized who he was. "The man from the cave. The man who bit me, you're him, aren't you? Stay away from me. I want this fucking door open right now or I swear to Christ that I will kill you."

"I didn't mean...I would never harm you, Cade. Let me explain. I was hurt and hungry and—"

"And what? I just happened to be a convenient cow to drain? And you did hurt me. You bit me and took my blood. Now open this fucking door."

When he reached toward her she nearly screamed, but he only keyed in the code to open the door. When she heard the latch disengage she threw open the door and made a dash into the hall. It was massive and when she turned back to him he pointed to the right and she took off to the left. Trust was not big on her list of things to give this man. Of course she had to turn back at the end of the hallway and go the way he had indicated first. It took her three more wrong turns before she made it to the top of the long stairs. When she opened the door at the top she nearly fell into the lap of Mr. MacManus who was just on the other side.

"Cade? Is everything all right? Is Shawn all right? I was just coming down to check on you two." Sara walked in the room then.

"I don't know who...that man's name is Shawn? You put me in a room with a stranger? What kind of sick people are you? He bit me. You told me I wouldn't come to any harm if I worked for you. You lied! But then I suppose that's what I should expect. No one tells me the truth. I'm leaving. If you contact me again, I'll...I'll...just don't contact me."

She was moving toward the kitchen when Sara was suddenly in front of her. Cade didn't think, she just reacted and pushed her hard with her mind. Sara banged hard against the wall and Cade kept going. She was outside and next to her bike when she realized she was still in his t-shirt and nothing else but her panties. Dropping to the hard concrete, she burst into tears.

Someone came up behind her, but she didn't need to look to know who it was. Mr. MacManus didn't touch her, but stood there with a blanket. She reached up, took it from him, and wrapped it around her body.

"Will you come into the house and let me explain? I'm sorry about what happened. I wasn't aware that Shawn hadn't told you anything when he marked you. You are safe here. I caused you no harm, Cade."

"Safe? Do you have any idea how stupid that word sounds coming from your mouth? I just want to leave. Please. I...that man, he and I, we...it was overwhelming and we had...when he bit me, we had sex. I don't even know him. I'm never—I've never done anything like that before."

"I believe you. Come into the house and let us explain. Please, it's cold out here and the children are worried about you."

His voice was soft, but there was something there. A tone, she supposed, and she nearly gave into it, nearly went into the house because he was commanding her to. But she wanted to go home, leave before it was too late. She wasn't sure too late for what and almost thought it was already too late, but fought his pull. Standing up she handed him the blanket.

"No. I don't know what you're trying to do, but I don't like to be told what someone else thinks is best for me. I'll be back tomorrow to finish out the work for you. I don't quit no matter how much weird shit goes on. Besides, I really need the money. Keep that man away from me, Mr. MacManus. We had a deal and I expect you to hold up your end of the bargain."

She knew it was going to be freezing riding home. She would probably get sicker, but there was no way she was going back into that house for her clothes. Aaron pulled his suit coat off and handed it toward her. She nearly took it then thought he may have some sort of tracking device in it. Paranoid? Yes, but she was willing to bet he could already track her somehow. Without a word she threw her leg over the seat and prayed the thing would start. When it did she turned it around and drove down the long drive. The cold was biting into her skin and her teeth were chattering when she got to the main road, but she didn't stop as she headed over to the bar. Sleeping there tonight seemed a smart idea.

She was standing at the stove when Paul came back to tell her she had a phone call. He normally just screamed at her to get it. Tonight he walked into her kitchen. She just knew that she didn't want to answer it.

"Paul, why don't you just tell them to quit calling here? I would be very happy if you did. I don't want to talk to whoever is on the other end. I don't care if they're telling me I've won the lottery."

"It's a woman. She sounds really upset. I tried to lie to her and tell her you weren't here and she said to put you on. Told me to tell you that she would either talk to you on the phone or come down here and speak to you. And I didn't want her to come here."

"Fuck! Will you get a number for me? Tell her I have six orders on the grill and I need this job too. Tell her I'll call her back before eleven. And tell her that I promise and I keep mine. If she has a problem with that, then tell her I quit."

Paul went to the phone to relay her message. Cade wanted to cry. That and she really wanted to go upstairs and take a long, hot bath, crawl into bed, and never wake up. About an hour ago her throat had started to hurt and now it was a full blown ache. Her muscles felt like someone had stretched her out on a rack and pulled her taut for several days, and her head was pounding like a jackhammer was being used in it. She couldn't afford to get sick.

At a quarter till eleven she called the number Paul had written down for her. She was on break and really wanted to lie down, but didn't figure Mrs. MacManus would be put off. On the second ring, she answered.

"I didn't think you'd call back. I was just putting on my coat to come down there and kick your ass. I need to speak to you."

"Yeah, I got that. Don't threaten my boss again. Long after I finish helping you out I still have to work here. What do you want? I have to get back to work soon." She sneezed three times and had to blow her nose while she delivered her little speech.

"You're sick. Come to the house after work tonight. Better yet, let me have someone come and get you. You can't be riding that bike around in this weather. You've probably gotten pneumonia or something worse. I'll have Aaron there when you get off."

"Gee, thanks, Mom. Whatever would I do without your loving care? Fuck off. I'm not going anywhere with you people. Hiring me to help out while your cook is gone does not make you my keepers. If this is all you wanted then I'm busy. I'll be there in the morning."

Cade was just about to hang up when she heard her name. She needed a nap not this woman. Bringing the phone back to her ear, she waited. Paul brought her a cup of tea and a bourbon chaser and set it in front of her. She grinned at him when he winked.

"I want to know what you are going to do about Shawn. I can talk to you about it tomorrow if you'd like to think about it. I know you are new to the idea of vampires, but they have needs and I would like it if you'd let me explain it to you."

"No. I don't want anything to do with that man. My break is over. I'll see you in the morning." Cade hung up and sat there.

"You okay, kid? Never seen you so upset before. Maybe you should quit them folks and keep away from them. That woman sounds like a real piece of work."

"You have no idea. I need the money or I would. I don't quit, you know that. Paul, do you think it would be all right if I could borrow fifty bucks from you until payday? I need to pay off someone and I think I need to get something for this cold. I'm good for it."

He gave her seventy, all the cash he had on him, and told her not to worry about it. She was a good kid and he liked her, he told her. Nearly crying again Cade went back to the kitchen and started on the three orders that were hanging there. She hadn't bothered asking him about the rooms upstairs. Paul's brother had flown in from out of town and he had moved in for a few weeks. Cade was sleeping in the cave whether she wanted to or not. At one-thirty he sent her home. A short freezing ride to the store and by two-forty-five she was back in the cave.

~~~

"The wound has a bit of silver in it. I think once we get it flushed out it should heal properly. Nasty business, head wounds, even for a vamp. Say, you can't remember anything, right? Well, this should help with that too."

Thomas Reilly, a vampire and a doctor, had examined his head shortly after Cade left the bar. Now he and Aaron were going to open the wound again and flush it out. While they set about preparing to do that Shawn thought about the woman, Cade.

Aaron had been livid when he came in from talking to her. Shawn grinned at that. He guessed livid had been an understatement. He had been furious that she wouldn't bow down to his wishes and even more so that she had so easily thrown off his edict. Then he had started on him.

"She didn't even know your name. She doesn't have a clue what it means now that you've bonded with her and she was strong enough to not only throw off my command, but to toss my mate across the room as if she was nothing more than a speck of dust."

"Aaron, I told you it was my fault. I should have been prepared for her magic. She does have telepathic powers anyway and with Shawn's blood it's only made them and her stronger."

Shawn nearly laughed when Aaron turned on Sara, but he decided that he might live longer if he didn't. He had never met two more headstrong people than Sara and Aaron. "Things have gotten out of hand with Cade. It's entirely my fault. When I came across her in that cave I had no idea that she was anything more than a—"

"Cave! Are you telling me she is living in a cave? In the wild? Christ, will there ever be a female that comes to this Kiss that isn't out to drive me insane! I thought when we heard that she was only living above the restaurant that she might have an apartment or an abandoned building she was staying in, but a cave. I want you to go and get her right now. Bring her back to this house and make her stay." Aaron was standing with his arms over his chest and looking for all the world like he would be obeyed when Shawn had another memory.

"You did that when we were in the French army together. You were mad because you couldn't get that twit of a commanding officer to listen to you when you told him that we were going to be attacked. We left that night and the next morning all the men, including the commander, were killed by the ambush. We let them think we, too, had been killed to change our existence."

"Yes, that's right. That's when we met Kyle. He had been turned and didn't know what the hell had happened. We sort of took him under our wing and helped him out. Do you remember Kyle, Shawn?"

"Kyle Dixon. He is...he's still alive. I heard from him just after I talked to you about coming here. He told me he is mated too. His mate is Madeline or something like that."

"It's Madison. That's great. I'm calling Thomas. He needs to get over here and look at this. This is great. But it still doesn't negate that you fucked up royally with this woman. You will fix this, Shawn."

And that was why he was laying here on the bed about to have his head sliced open again and then cleaned. He wished it were that easy to erase things. He didn't think he'd ever forget the look on Cade's face when he'd reached beyond her to unlock the door. She'd looked terrified of him.

CHAPTER 6

Cade got up at five and thought she might just chance Sara's wrath. Her entire body was on fire one minute and freezing the next. It hadn't helped that when she got to the cave all of her things were wet. Even the floor was damp. She didn't have the energy to start a fire and didn't have anything dry to keep it going with. Moving slowly, she made her way to the bike, not caring if it started on not. Or even if it fell on top of her and crushed her.

When she pulled into the big drive at the house she sat on the bike for a little while. There was no way she could work. There wasn't any way she would be able to deal with Mrs. MacManus either. Leaving her things on the bike, she went to the door to knock. When Mrs. MacManus opened it, before she had the chance, Cade nearly tumbled in the house on top of her.

"You're sick. Come in before you pass out. Did you spend the night in that cave again? Aaron! Shawn! Someone come help me. Cade, can you hear me?"

"If you'd shut up and give me a chance to answer any of your questions, I'd tell you. And how did you know about...the man? Never mind. I've come to tell you I'm too sick to work today. Dock me, I don't care. I'm going back to bed."

Before she could turn and get back on her bike she was scooped up in someone's arms. She squealed when she was suddenly in the same bedroom from last night. The man holding her looked no less pleased to be holding her than she felt.

"Put me down. Are you nuts? Well that was a stupid question, wasn't it? If you don't put me down this instant I'm going to call the police." Then she was suddenly airborne and landing with a bounce on the bed again. Before she could move off of it he had her pinned there with her hands over her head and his body over her.

"Hush. You do go on, don't you? Now, I'm going to get up and you're going to stay here. If you don't, I'm going to tie you here. Do I make myself clear?

"You'd better hope you can tie me faster than I can move because when I get up I'm going to bash your head in. Why does everyone in this house treat me as if I'm five? I wasn't staying. I'm going back to bed as soon as I leave here. Now, get off me, you big oaf."

She tried to throw him off with her legs and he pressed her into the bed. She stilled when she felt his erection pressing against her hip. She turned her head away from him and started crying. She didn't have the energy to fight him and she didn't feel good. He started talking to her softly.

"I know that you've had a lot thrown at you. I'm sorry for that. I'm not sorry I found you or what you are to me. My name is Shawn Alan MacFarland. I was born in the early part of the third century. I've been friends with Aaron since the late twelfth century when we were pressed into service to fight. My memory was lost over two weeks ago when someone, and I don't know who or why yet, led me out of a bar and ambushed me. Thomas Reilly, a doctor for our kind, opened the wound to my head late last night and cleaned it out. There was silver in it. He doesn't know if it was put there on purpose or if it was an accident. I've been remembering bits and pieces since then, but big chunks of my life are gone right now. You, however, are very fresh in my mind."

She didn't say anything to that. She wasn't sure what she could say to a man who claimed he was sixteen hundred years old. There was no way that any of this could be real.

"Are you going to let me go? I don't want to be here and you can't make me stay. I know I keep saying that, but you really can't." She hoped.

"Sara said that you know very little about our kind. Do you know what it is to be bonded and mated to a vampire? Or what happens when you are bonded to one?"

"No, and frankly I could give a good two shits. I want you to let me go, Mr. MacFarland. I've had about enough of this and you people."

"My name is Shawn, Cade. I've had my cock buried deep inside of you. We are well past the point of you calling me Mr. anything. To be bonded, a vampire must exchange blood with his mate. And to be mated, we would exchange blood during sex, while we're climaxing. You would drink from me and me from you.

Sometimes, if the mate has fangs she can bite back, but if not, a cut is made over the heart of the vampire and you would drink from there. I would drink from your wrist. It makes us one, bringing our combined powers to each other and we would be able to speak through our minds. You and I already have that ability, but with the exchange it would be stronger and over a greater distance. As a vampire of my age I don't need to feed as often or as long as a younger vampire, but I still need blood. A mated couple drinks from each other only. Unless one of them is a master. He can turn a human by taking nearly all of his or her blood and giving that one his. If he is mated, then his mate would help in the conversion and that human turned vampire would be their child."

She looked up at him. "We've never done that. I've never had your blood and I'm never going to either. Also, you've drank from me, but not while we were...when we had sex. So what does this have to do with me?"

"We have exchanged blood, Cade. When I drank from you in the cave I didn't seal the wound and you had lost a great deal of blood. When you came here yesterday morning you passed out and Aaron was going to turn you rather than let you die. I came just in time to stop him from giving you his blood. I gave you mine instead. My blood healed you and made you stronger."

"No, no that's not right. I was sick, getting a cold. I had lost some blood, but not that much. I didn't need your blood. Take it back."

"I had drunk deeply from you too, remember? I was half starved and when I sank my teeth into you I drank too deep and then left the wound unattended. You were near death when I gave you my blood. I can't take it back, love, and I don't want to at any rate. You're my mate and we have gone far enough with the process that I can only feed from you. If you refuse me, then I die."

At some point he had released her arms and he now held her. She was tired and dizzy. Her body wanted to snuggle up to his and stay there. Then something occurred to her.

"Since we haven't...the last thing, the sex thing, you can drink from somebody else still, right? You don't need me now. You can find someone else, right?"

"No. Feeding from another would kill me at this point. It's your blood my body needs now and no one else's will do. You are my mate, Cade. I will spend our lives taking care of you, providing for you, and making your life easier. It's my duty."

"I don't want you to do any of those things. I can do them on my own. I want to do them on my own. Please, don't you understand? You have to take it back. I want you to take it back."

She started sobbing again and couldn't seem to stop. Shawn held her close and, as much as she wanted to tell him to let her go, it was comforting and warm. It wasn't long before she was asleep.

When she opened her eyes he was staring down at her. She didn't know how long she had been out, but if his beard was any indication, it had been at least a day or more. She knew nothing about men's grooming habits. The few men she had known as an adult had shaved daily and so she didn't know what happened when they didn't. Did facial hair grow slow, fast?

Before she could stop herself she reached up and rubbed the back of her hand over his whiskers. They were firm, but not hard like she thought they'd be. When he didn't move she ran her thumb over his lips and watched as they pinked up a little. His eyes had been a deep blue when she first looked at him and now they were turning red, a deep blood red. And his fangs peeked out over his bottom lip. For reasons she couldn't fathom she continued her exploration. His cheeks were next; they were high and tight and there was a small scar just below his left eye. She looked at it then ran her finger over it and then looked at him again.

"A piece of shrapnel hit me when a blast went off too close to where I was sleeping. I was lucky that I didn't lose my eye, or anything else." His voice was soft and gentle.

Satisfied, Cade ran her fingers through his hair and felt the small knot at the back of his head. She didn't do anything more than brush her fingers over it lightly, but he still winced. His hair was soft and silky. She was amazed at how thick it was, and curly. It was a deep brown with hundreds of highlights in it of every color she could think of. The whiskers on his face were blonder, more golden browns than reds. And it was not as long as she had first thought, just past his shoulders. She thought it had been tied back before. She liked it better down.

Shifting on the bed so that she was facing him she ran her hand down his neck, pausing at the beating pulse in his throat. She watched mesmerized as it sped up with her touch and then more when she ran her thumb over it. His swift intake of breath had her look up at him again, but he only nodded. She wasn't sure what he meant, but took it to mean she could continue.

Never had Cade touched a man like this, or anyone for that matter. His skin was both hot and cool to her touch. Firm and soft in places she didn't think possible. His chest was hard, his breast muscles were taut with strength yet she wasn't afraid he'd hurt her. When she touched his nipple it puckered and hardened, the areola around it crinkled too. Not really giving much thought to what she was doing, she leaned forward and licked at the hard nub and then nipped it gently with her teeth. Her whole body tightened when he growled at her. The rumbling came through her hand, which was still on his chest. Afraid to look at him now, she nipped again and then pulled it into her mouth and suckled. When his hand cupped the back of her head and held her there she opened her mouth over him and sucked more of his skin into her mouth. Her body flooded with cream.

"Cade, baby, don't stop touching me. Please, I want you to touch me. Explore me."

When he rolled to his back, taking her with him, she slid her leg over his and then moved to sit astride him. Her legs wrapped to either side of his waist. He didn't touch her other than to adjust her over his abdomen. Now she had both hands free to touch.

His ribs were muscled and, when she felt them ripple under her touch, she reached under her shirt and felt her own. Hers were so different than his. She used both hands, one to touch him and the other to feel the difference between the two of them.

"My ribs are thicker than yours. My skin isn't as toned. You have a scar here too. It feels long and like you might have really been hurt."

"Before I was changed, the reason I was changed I guess. I was twenty-seven and had fallen over a cliff. The woman who found me changed me. She said that she needed a companion and thought I'd do. She thought I was handsome enough to satisfy her through the years. I don't think she thought I'd last this long. She died some years later. Another lover took her and staked her in the sun."

"Did you? Satisfy her, I mean?" She hoped he wouldn't comment on the tone. It sounded like she was jealous, which she was not.

"She didn't complain. At least not about that part of our relationship anyway. She seemed to think I belonged to her and I thought I should be my own man. I wonder how I can remember this and nothing that happened last week."

"Maybe she meant more to you than you realized. I'm finished. I'd like to go now, please. I have to work at the bar tonight as a bartender."

She started to roll off him, hurt at something, though she refused to acknowledge what. She was just swinging her leg off him when he rolled and trapped her beneath him again.

"My turn. But I want to start here. I've thought about your breasts. They're larger than I thought they'd be. I never got the chance to really taste them before, but I would like to now."

Without waiting for her to tell him no he ripped the shirt from the neckline to the hem, tearing her bra from her as well. She felt her nipples harden and her breasts tighten as his had done when she had touched them. Her breathing became harder too; she tried to blame it on his weight on her, but knew it to be from his body on her, not the weight. When he ran his thumb up under their weight, she closed her eyes against the heat that surged through her.

"Watch me, Cade, like I did you. I want you to watch me as I touch you. You have beautiful breasts. They're full and heavy. Their soft weight just fits in my hands and your nipples are so responsive."

Watching his head lower to her breasts she couldn't take her eyes off of his. When his tongue swiped over the hard peak she felt her pussy gush more liquid. When she tried to close her thighs he reached down and ran his hand down her thigh to her calf. Lifting it, he put her foot at his hip and opened her to him. Her pussy heated at the feel of his cock at her clit.

"Don't rush me. I want to touch so much more of you. I can smell your arousal, Cade. The spicy heat that calls to me. It's everything I can do not to move down your body and bury my face over you and feast. I will, but not right now. First, I want to suckle at your breasts as you did mine. Next time, love, do it longer. I've never known my nipples to be so sensitive before. Your hot little mouth nearly made me come when you bit me."

His head lowered to her breasts and when his tongue worried her nipple only she rocked up to him, begging him to take more. His chuckle only made her needier and wetter. Wrapping her other foot over his hip she locked her ankles around him and rocked into him.

"Please. I need you to make me come. I need to come, Shawn." Rocking again, she nearly screamed at him when he pressed her harder into the bed, stopping her from moving.

"I'm not going to be rushed, Cade. Trust me. The wait will make it so much better. I'm going eat your pussy now. And if you're a good girl I'll let you come in my mouth. I want you to flood my mouth with your come."

Shawn moved down her body, nipping and kissing her. With every touch of his mouth to her skin she felt a flame ignite there, a heat so hot she knew she'd have scorch marks from his mouth alone.

Cade didn't have to be told her panties were soaked. She could feel the moisture running down her ass and pooling beneath her. When he grabbed the strings at the sides of her panties she was panting. When he didn't move she sat up and looked at him. Her legs were on either side of his massive forearms as he rested his body weight on them. He was smiling at her, a predatory smile that made her heart leap and her pussy spasm. His fangs were long and sharp and the thought of them sinking into her, into her pussy, made her moan with need. While she watched he ripped the material from her hips and lowered his head to her opening.

The first time his tongue touched her she moved up into him. He spread her open by bringing his hands under her thighs and then curling them around her. He opened her legs further and then lifted her up. She couldn't move as much anymore. And when he brought his fingers down closer to her pussy and pulled her open more he started fucking her deep with his tongue. The world narrowed and centered on him and what he was doing to her.

A man had never gone down on her before. The few times she'd had sex it had been quick and unsatisfying. Cade didn't think it would ever be anything but spectacular with Shawn. As soon as he sucked her clit into his mouth and began to work it with his tongue he slipped his hand under her, pressed one finger into her pussy, and began pumping her as he worked her. She was riding him now. Her hips moved as much as he would allow them up and down his fingers and his tongue. Grabbing the sheet beneath her she held it, hoping that when the moment came when she climaxed she wouldn't fly off and shatter. When a second then third finger entered her she began sobbing and moaning, begging him. Begging him to give her relief, to give her what she knew he and only he could give her.

"Come for me, Cade. Let me have your nectar. Let me take your honey into me. Let me feel it slide from your hot pussy and down the back of my throat."

Her release was an explosion. There was no build up of it, only Shawn telling her to come and she did. She felt her pussy flood his mouth, felt him lap and lap it up, and felt him swallow her juices. And when he slipped his finger into her tiny hole at her ass, she came again, screaming out his name over and over as he took her higher and higher. When she started to come down he slipped out of her and she whimpered at the loss.

His mouth covered hers and she could feel the wetness on him. Her juices covered his mouth and lips. Licking at the taste she groaned and pulled his lip into her mouth to taste more. His cock pressed at her opening and she lifted her legs and wrapped them around him as he rocked deep into her. She came again as his cock began to piston into her. She sank her nails into his ribs and pulled him down so that her nipples rubbed his chest. When he nuzzled her neck there was no thought to stopping him. She wanted his bite, wanted to feel his teeth slide into her flesh, and when his tongue soothed the area and he plunged them into her, she came again. Her pussy began pulling him deeper, pulling him closer even as she felt him stiffen. When the first splash of his cum sprayed inside of her she screamed out his name again, sobbing and holding on to him. As he dropped onto her she fell into unconsciousness knowing that things would never be the same again.

CHAPTER 7

Sleep eluded him. Shawn watched Cade lay beside him and wondered how he could have been so lucky as to find her the way that he had. A string of events had brought her into his life and though he couldn't remember them, at least not in great detail, he knew it was fated that he be in that bar at that time.

He had worn her out and knew that she would sleep for a while longer. The whisker burns on her neck matched the ones on her thighs. He couldn't help but feel proud about them. If he could have gone out and howled he would have. His mark at her throat was there too. And would remain as long as she didn't drink from him to bond.

He had thought to give her his wrist tonight when they'd made love, but didn't want her to turn him down. He knew that she would have, too. For now, as long as she stayed with him, he could live with her not taking the final step. It would make her vulnerable to other males who wanted to feed from her, but his mark should keep most of those away. Shawn was a powerful vampire; his age alone gave him powers that others never obtained.

As much as he wanted to stay with her he needed to talk to Aaron. Another memory of that night came to him when she was touching him. Her touch. It had been so soothing and so soft and he had never been so aroused in his life. Just thinking about her finger on his nipples, her mouth opening over him made his cock harden again.

Going into the bathroom he showered. He knew that Aaron would know that they had had sex and he would also know that they had not yet bonded, but he still showered and shaved. He would be more careful in the future about that. He didn't want to make her too sore when he rubbed against her. Stopping by the big bed before he left the room he leaned down and kissed her gently. Her moan and small smile did a lot for his mood as he left the bedroom whistling. He found his friend in the study with the door closed.

"Is she better? You took her away so quickly that I wasn't sure if she had been injured or something else had happened to her. I take it she is a little more receptive of you."

Aaron had never been one to beat around the bush. Shawn laughed. He was remembering more about their friendship too. They had indeed been friends for more centuries than most vamps lived. He wondered why he had been coming here. He knew there was a reason and hoped that Aaron could tell him.

"She had a fever and the beginnings of pneumonia. A small sip that she isn't even aware of and she's better. And yes, you nosey old man, she and I are making headway into our relationship. She won't bond with me. Not yet anyway. I don't...I think it's better if she makes the decision on this. I know the risks, but if I force her I feel I'll regret it. Understand?"

"Yes. She's very independent. And you're right, it is risky. Especially with her as headstrong as she is. I wouldn't put it past her to run out into the rain again just to prove you wrong about you healing her. Don't get me wrong, I love strong women. Sara is the strongest willed woman I know. But I tell you, sometimes I want to beat her ass so badly that I can't think straight. And if you tell her that, I'll deny it."

There was no denying the love between those two. The household could feel it as well. Their children were happy and healthy and not a little like them both. And Shawn had known Duncan since he'd been with Aaron. He had been his servant since he'd saved Aaron's life and Aaron his many more years ago than anyone would guess.

"Aaron, can you tell me why was I coming here? According to my driver's license I don't live in Ohio. I had to have a reason for coming all this way to see you. I know we're friends, but something brought me here, didn't it?"

"You didn't tell me. You called three weeks ago and said you needed to talk to me about something. You told me that you were having issues with the master there and that you needed my advice. I had hoped that you were coming to ask me to be your second or that you wanted to join me here. I think you would make an excellent master, by the way."

Shawn got up to pace. Something nudged at his mind so he tried to relax and let it come. He had something else to ask while that thought stewed around a bit. "The woman who I was leaving the bar with, her name was Dana Simpson. I don't know why that seems important, but it won't quit tickling my mind. Does it ring any bells with you? And my cell phone is missing. I'm not sure what that has to do with anything, but neither my money nor the credit cards have been touched."

When Aaron reached into his pocket and pulled out his phone Shawn only half listened as he talked to someone named Pete. He assumed it was another of his Kiss and a female because they were making fun of her mate Dominic.

"Yes, tell him I said that's the way it goes. Now, the reason I called. I have a name I need you to search for me...yes, it's for Shawn...Dana Simpson...I doubt they exchanged the spelling of her name, Pete." He turned to Shawn. "She wants to know if you remember a physical description. Anything you remember so that if she pulled a picture up she'd be able to narrow it down for you."

"Dark hair, black, straight. Not too tall, about five-foot-five at best. Smallish frame, her eyes where green—dark green that had sparks in them. I have no idea why I know this. It just came to me when you asked." Another thing came to him. "She wasn't alone. A man, dark-skinned, though I wouldn't say African American. More like he was browned, he was a shifter. Tall as me, but not as muscled, bulkier but not fat. He...I think he hit me with a whip of chain. Yeah, a chain. I can't remember...there was something he wanted."

"Are you getting this, Pete? Yes, I'll tell him...no, I don't think I will, but I'll give him the option...thank you, love. Tell Dominic I said to shut up and bear it. We all have to."

Shawn sat down. His head was pounding again and he could feel that there was something huge he was just about to remember. He was rubbing his head when he felt the shimmer of magic come into the room.

"Hello, Aaron. You must be Shawn. Hummm, mated to a Lesser faerie, are you? Good for you. They are the favorite of my beings. Well, the Lesser ones are sort of a pain in the ass. And they are a stubborn lot too. But they are the only ones who stood by me when Sherman was trying to have me taken out of commission."

"Shawn, this is Mel. She's Sara's cousin and the Queen of Molavonta, Mistress of Light, Keeper of All Magic, yada yada. She pops in whenever it suits her and knows no boundaries whatsoever. Watch her, she'll come into your chamber without so much as a knock on the door."

"Aaron, you know that I only did that once. And the way you and Sara go at it like rabbits it's a small wonder you two don't have enough vamps to drain the world. Pay him no mind. I could feel the magic between you and your mate. She gives off a certain magic and I've been looking for her sire and dame first before I approach her."

"She's not a horse, Mel. Stop quoting that stupid show you continue to watch with Duncan. Hello, Aaron. I'm happy to see you've found your friend. My name is James, by the way. I'm Mel's grandfather. Though there are days when she makes me wish I was her father and could take a switch to her arse."

Shawn couldn't help it, he burst out laughing. Looking at Aaron made him laugh harder. The man looked ready to pop a vessel. He wondered if this happened a lot and then realized that it did. Beings coming and going at will must be hard on him. Then he realized what the queen had said.

"Wait! You said I was mated to a faerie? Cade is a faerie? How did that happen?" He sat down hard after he had gotten up when the man and woman had entered the room.

"Oh well, faerie sex is really quite complicated. They have to be in flight, you see. And their wings must be back. So the trick is to fly very high in the sky then as they have sex, they begin to fall. It's quite beautiful. Unless of course—"

"I think he meant, 'how do you know she's a faerie?' not how she came to be born one. Sometimes, James, I'm sure you do that on purpose. Why on earth would you even know how fairies have sex? You know, never mind. I don't even want to know how you know," Aaron said shaking his head.

"He follows everything around until they have no choice but to have sex while he's watching. He doesn't give them any peace until he knows. Hello, darling, how are you this fine evening? I'm Savannah, Mel's mother."

Shawn kissed the woman's hand and bowed before the man. He knew that they were a royal couple, and they held themselves as such. His head hurt less and he wondered if it was the distraction that was helping. "I'm Shawn. So this is a pastime of yours, to follow around woodland creatures until they've no choice but to have sex with you watching or not? Sounds like a strange hobby if you ask me."

"Oh, Lesser fairies have their use. I've seen them rally together and take on something ten times their power and size. Mari and Genese, two of the flower fairies, have mated with Lesser. Your mate is only half faerie. Can't figure out yet what else she is. Not until I have a talk with her." Shawn watched as the man pulled out a huge book from the air.

He wondered what it was when he saw the title, Magical Creatures, and then the drawing on the front was a hodge podge of creatures and beings. Fairies were there, as was a centaur; a dragon took up most of the top of the page. As he continued to look Shawn could see beings in the grass, among the trees, and a few in clusters that looked like they made up a flower and its petals. The drawing was elaborate and in great detail. When Savannah sat next to him Shawn looked at her in surprise.

"Aaron tells me you've lost some of your memories. That would be a sad thing, I think. But you'll get them back. I know a bit about you, well, actually I know a great deal about you, but only bits can I tell you. You're very old, one of the oldest vampires alive as a matter of fact. You want to know why you're here, correct?"

"Yes, I was coming here for a reason. I don't know why, but I feel it might be important as to why I was ambushed outside of the bar. Do you know why I'm here?"

Shawn wasn't sure why he knew, but he was reasonably sure that this woman knew everything, including who the woman was that had caused him harm. He wanted her to tell him, but also knew that she wouldn't. He was just settling back against the sofa when he felt Cade coming toward him. He looked to the doorway just as she stepped through.

~~~

Cade felt the tingle she always did when she was on an assignment. She never understood what it was; just that it had saved her enough times that she didn't ignore it. Stepping through the door, her eyes collided with Shawn's and her breath caught. When he stood she backed up a step before she caught herself.

"I'm leaving now. I'd like...I had different clothes and I'd like them back please. I can't keep coming here and leaving with less of them. I don't have the money to keep replacing them."

"Cade, I told you that I would—"

"You'd better think very hard on how much damage I'll do to you if you finish that statement. I told you before that I live my own life. If you want to...eat, you can call and I'll do what you need to be done. I won't be responsible for your death just because you're a pig. Now, I'd like my clothes, damn it."

Cade felt stupid and childish. But she'd had enough of these people. She was sure that in their minds they were doing what was best for her, but she had a life and it had been just fine until Shawn showed up in her cave. Duncan cleared his throat behind her and when she turned he handed her freshly laundered clothes. With a kiss to his cheek she went to the bathroom he'd pointed to and changed. When she came out, surprise, surprise, there stood not one, but two men who she would just as soon hit before speaking to.

"Cade, you have to know how dangerous it is for you to be out alone in the night. Stay here tonight and I'll make you other arrangements in the morning. You'll be safe and I'll feel better about one of my own."

"Fuck off," was her answer to Mr. MacManus when he made his statement. She walked over to the stairs, sat on the bottom one, and started to lace up her boots. Cade didn't care anymore. She'd made Shawn a deal. If he chose not to take it, then so be it.

"Now see here. You are a guest in my home and—"

"Guest! Christ, are you flipping kidding me? I was leaving on my own. Then suddenly your...what did you call her? Your mate yells for help and I'm in bed with a man I know nothing about. And you!" she turned toward Shawn. "I'm just a regular person trying to make it and you invade my space and bite—"

"You were living in a cave! I—"

"Don't you dare preach to me as to where I live, coffin boy! And you may speak when I'm finished. Where was I? Oh yeah, you come into my home and bite me. And not only did you bite me, but you didn't fix it so I wouldn't bleed to death in the process. Now I will admit that I didn't stop you from having sex with me at that time, but no more. You need to have dinner then you call me and I'll meet you somewhere. Otherwise, stay the fuck away from me, both of you."

Cade stormed to the front door only to turn sharply and move on to the kitchen. She picked up her bag and her jacket and went out the door. Duncan winked at her when she kissed his cheek. When her bike started the first try she felt like someone was looking down on her and she left the estate.

CHAPTER 8

The diner was busy and when Paul told her she had a phone call she stomped to the phone and snarled her name. The quiet at the other end didn't bother her as much as she thought it should have. Cade had had a really shitty week and it wasn't getting any better with this interruption.

"You were supposed to call me back. I'm fucking sick and tired of this bullshit, Cade. I told you that—"

Cade put the receiver in the cradle. She didn't slam it down on Gabriel like she so wanted to, but simply dropped it gently on the hook. Then she waited for it to ring again.

"Paul's Place. How may I help you tonight?" She didn't even try to disguise her voice or take any of her pent up bad mood out of her tone. Gabriel didn't care, he was pissed too. His next words told her that.

"How would you like it if I sent two thugs to Paul's house and had them rape his little girl and fuck his wife until she can't walk? You think that hanging up on me gets you any points with me? You'll fucking regret it if you try that shit again. You are going to listen to me or so help me, you and everyone you know will pay for it."

Cade looked at Paul standing by the bar. He looked so content and happy. He loved his wife and daughter and she knew that if anything happened to them she'd never forgive herself. She turned her back to the man who had always been there for her.

"I fucking hate you. Not that I think there will ever be a time when I don't, but right now I could gladly put a cross hair on your forehead and blow your fucking brains out. Send the information to the usual place. And if half the money isn't with the information then you'd better find the deepest hole you can and stay there and pray I don't ever find you."

This time when she hung up Cade did slam the phone down. Tears of hate and frustration clouded her vision as she walked to the ladies room to freshen up. This was perhaps one of the worst weeks she'd ever had and now this. She didn't think it could get much worse. Then she walked out of the bathroom. And there stood another of her life's major crises. Her step-brother, Garrett Reid.

"I need to talk to you, Caddy. I need money really bad or they're gonna kill me for sure. Just a thousand. That should be enough to hold them off until you can get the rest. How long will it take you to raise the other ten grand?"

"I don't have it. And even if I did you wouldn't be getting it. I told you last time you borrowed money from me if you didn't pay me back then never again. I'm finished helping you. I'm neither your ATM nor your mother, thank God. Now, go away."

Cade had been giving money to her family in one way or another since she'd left home. She wasn't saying they were the main reason she lived like she did, but they were the biggest reason. When she'd left home eight years ago it had been because she wanted to hide from people like Gabriel.

"You owe me, Cade. Now I need that money and you'll get it for me. So help me to Christ, I'm fucking sick of you telling me no all the time."

Garrett's fist came out before she could dodge it. It was just as well, she supposed. She couldn't hit him back anyway. She had been taught by another man's fist that she was never to hit her "poor younger brother". He had issues. He had problems that made him like he was. Yeah, he had problems all right, a temper that was lethal and fists to back it up.

Cade may not have been able to hit him, but Paul had no such restraints. His bat nearly connected with Garrett's head before the younger man could get out the door. Paul was helping her up off the floor before she realized where she was. And she had never been able to figure out what he thought she owed him for. He said that to her every time he asked for money. When she asked about it, his reply was always the same, "you just do."

"Why don't you just hit him, girl? I've seen you take on a man twice the size of that skinny one's ass and come out on top. Why him? What makes him so special?"

Cade wanted to say nothing, but that would only make it worst. She told him she couldn't hit him because of his mental issues and left it at that. She spent the rest of the night holding a bag of ice to her head between orders. It was eleven-thirty before she was able to go out to her bike, which of course didn't start, and then trudge the seven miles to her cave. It was nearly two before she was able to lie down and another hour after that before she fell asleep. A short hour and a half later she was up again.

Duncan let her in the house at five after five. With a mumbled, "sorry I'm late," she set to work. The kids had requested a big breakfast this morning and she was starting on the potatoes when Aaron walked in.

Cade was surprised he didn't start on her right away. But then she kept her back to him for twenty minutes before Sara and Shawn walked in. Cracking two eggs into a bowl to scramble she heard someone's sharp intake of breath and then Shawn was pulling her face around to meet his gaze.

"Who the hell hit...why do I smell blood? Are you hurt again? Christ, you need to be put into a padded room. Are you going to tell me who hit you or am I going to have to beat your ass to get it out of you?"

"Do you always resort to violence to get what you want? And I bet you wonder why you're as old as you are and still single. It's none of your business why I'm bleeding or who hit me. And the minute you think you can lay a hand on me in punishment I will hurt you in ways you can only imagine. Now, if you're done with the caveman bullshit, I have things to do."

Cade moved away from Shawn and pulled the biscuits from the oven just as the kids came into the kitchen. She ignored the adults and focused on the kids. It was difficult, but she thought she was doing very well.

"Okay, guys, here's your money. I hope you spend it well. You should both be proud of yourself."

"I didn't win. I tried really hard, but I didn't win. I'm not a nice person, am I, Cade? That's why you gave me that test to do, because you know I'm not a nice person."

Before Cade could answer Lizzy, her mother leapt to her daughter's defense. It might have been humorous if not for the fact that Cade didn't do anything wrong and that Shawn was trying to come between Cade and Sara. Even Cade knew one never stepped between two women fighting.

"What have you been telling my daughter? What do you mean telling her she's not a good person? She most certainly is."

Cade had had enough. It was Friday and she had been bitten, left to die, beat up, shit on, fucked senseless, punched, and yelled at enough for one week. She tossed the towel on the counter, slammed the money for the kids on the table, picked up her bag, and headed toward the door.

"I'm sorry, Duncan, but I can't finish up the two weeks. I hope you can forgive me. I just can't take all the issues this family has. I'll see you around."

Cade never made it out the door. Of course that didn't surprise her. She never even made it to the end of the long counter before she was pressed tightly against the cabinets, her body hanging there without a single person touching her. Now that surprised her.

"Mom, let her go. She didn't tell me that I'm a mean person. Please let her go and I'll tell you why I'm mean. Please, Mom?"

Cade didn't struggle. She hung there with the pressure of the magic, thinking that she couldn't fight it, was forbidden to fight it for some reason. When she was lowered to the floor, Cade picked up her things and went for the door again. Lizzy stopped her.

"Please don't go, Cade. I want you to hear what happened when I did what you asked, me to be nice. They were mean to me. Not really mean, but they made fun of me and kept asking me if I was sick. And the girl I was trying to be nice to, she kept running away from me. She thought I was trying to hurt her or make fun of her."

"What happened, baby? Why did Cade ask you to be nice to someone? Tell us from the beginning," Aaron asked his daughter as he pulled her into his lap.

"Lizzy, I really would like to leave. I've had a really sh...crappy week. You can tell your parents. I don't want to be here anymore."

"But you need to know. See, Mom, Cade told Mac if he got a B on his math test, she'd give him five dollars, then if he got an A, she'd give him ten. He got an A. I wanted to play too, but I do well on my tests anyway so she told me I had to be nice to three people."

"Lizzy, I'm sure you're nice to everyone. Why do you suppose Cade asked you to be nice to someone in the first place?"

When Duncan snorted everyone turned to look at him. "Miss Lizzy, you know the answer to that. You have not been nice to Miss Cade or Miss Penny for some time now. I would also need to point out that you have grown quiet fond of yourself as well. Why Miss Penny told you just the other day that you need to have your mouth cleaned with a soapy product when you gave her the mouth."

"Huh? Ah. Duncan, it's 'mouth washed out with soap,' and 'give her lip.' You really should get out more." Cade noticed that Duncan had issues with colloquialisms when she'd first met him. She thought it was funny most of the time, and hilarious the other times.

"Precisely. Miss Lizzy's mouth is dirty. And what happened when this other young miss found out you were trying to be nice to her? Did she not tell you that you were a 'snotty bitch?' I think Miss Cade had a brilliant idea. If her ladyship approves, I believe you should be put into a place where you must learn to curb your mouth."

Cade could see the temper rising on the little girl. Her cheeks getting red notwithstanding, she looked at Duncan like he was going to be her last meal. Just when Cade thought the room would explode Shawn threw back his head and laughed.

"Bloody hell, Aaron, she's your daughter! Remember the time you told me that you were going to make sure...maybe a tale for later. But by all that's holy, she's as stubborn and pigheaded as you are."

Cade felt his laughter curl around her body and tighten. She looked over at him when she felt his eyes touch her. Everything within her wanted to grab him up and press him against the nearest hard surface. Or better yet, for him to press against her. When his laughter stopped and he stood she backed up two steps then more as he advanced. "Stop! You need to back up. We are never going there again, you understand? Now move back right now."

"Your mouth says one thing, your body another. I can smell you, your need. You want me as much as I want you. Let me touch you, let me take you to the lair, Cade, and make love to you all day."

Cade closed her eyes and reached for him. "You have no idea what I want. If you had a clue you'd leave me alone. If you're not hungry, then go away." Turning to the others in the room she said, "I'll be back in an hour. I have to go to the Post Office." With that, she left.

The Post Office was busy. Cade didn't keep up with the holidays so had no idea if one was coming up or just ending. When the person in front of her moved out of the way Cade wanted to scream when the worker put up a "station closed" sign and left. But within a minute the next person, one she knew, came to the counter. Linda waved at Cade as she approached her.

"I heard you got a job at Paul's place. You like working for him? He has the best homemade apple pie I ever ate."

Cade had had Paul's apple pie, had even taken it out of the box and baked it for him, following the instructions on the box. She thought it was by and far the nastiest thing she'd ever eaten. But that was just her. She actually preferred cherry, but not out of a box.

"Yeah. He's a good guy. I like working in the kitchen. I think it keeps me out of trouble. I have a package to pick up. Is it in yet?"

"Yes. It was dropped off about an hour ago. You know, if you got yourself a P.O. Box you wouldn't have to wait in line to get your mail. I could set you up with one in no time."

Cade knew that. Linda told her that every time she came in to get her mail. She didn't want one in case someone asked questions she couldn't answer. Plus, filling out the application to have one required something she didn't have. A real address, that was.

"I don't get all that much mail anyway. My meds are the only thing I get delivered so it would just be silly to have something to worry about."

Cade had set up the insurance company sending her some sort of maintenance drug every so often as a reason to get the packages. When Linda handed Cade her package, she went out in the cool spring afternoon and sat on her bike. Pulling her metal detector out from under saddle bags she was happy to find that nothing metallic was inside and then opened the large white bag.

"Mother fuck." Gabriel had sent her money all right, but in the form of a check. What the hell was she supposed to do with an eighteen hundred dollar check that was made out to cash? That was going to be hard to explain. Stuffing it in the pocket of her jacket, Cade pulled out the file. She had less than five hours to find a laptop with Internet service. Starting her bike and pulling out onto the main roadway she decided that she really needed to get moving. When Gabriel started to threaten people she knew then it was time to move on. As she made her way back to the MacManus estate she read little pieces of the bio on her target at each stop light. By the time she reached the drive she knew as much as she could.

CHAPTER 9

Shawn was pacing his lair when he felt Cade return to the mansion. He could probably have gone up to her, but for some reason he knew that he might live longer if he stayed where he was. He thought about her fiery temper and grinned. She was a sight to behold when she was pissed off.

Shawn remembered more about why he'd come here. There was something between him and the other master. Shawn hadn't figured out what that was, but there was something really wrong there. He could also remember Aaron completely now. Even when they had met and how.

Shawn had been wandering through the streets of a little town in Ireland when he happened upon Duncan. Shawn could smell another vamp on the little man and was bored enough and curious enough to follow him back to a deep cave of sorts. He'd found Aaron, nearly starved and weak. It took several weeks, weeks of them talking and getting to know one another, for Shawn to show the ropes to both men. Duncan on how to be a servant of a vampire and Aaron on how to use his limited powers as a newly turned vampire. Even then Aaron had been a strong vampire. It didn't surprise Shawn in the least that he was now a powerful master.

When the need to sleep became too much to bear Shawn lay down on his bed. It still smelled of Cade and sex. He nearly went up to get her and bring her back to his bed, but again resisted. He needed to figure out how to handle a woman like her.

Sara had told him to back off. He was sure she meant well, but Cade needed someone to watch over her and to keep her safe. He realized that he'd not gotten from her what had happened to her face and who had hit her. He'd have to make a mental note on asking her about it the next time he saw her.

Sleep was weighing heavily on his mind when he thought of several things he wanted to ask Cade. There was the bruise first and foremost and then why she was living in a cave, also if she had any more powers than the few he'd already witnessed. He also should get her a more reliable car to drive. She couldn't be riding around on a bike in the dead of winter. As he closed his eyes a vision of her lying beneath him, moaning and begging him to let her come had him groan. He knew in that moment that his life was taking on a whole new spin.

~~~

Cade sat in the coffee/Internet café for a good hour before she touched the mouse. She'd known that she was wasting time, that she had to do what she'd been told or Gabriel would hurt Paul and his family. She wanted to scream she was so frustrated with herself. If she'd been a little smarter or a little savvier about things this may not be where she was right now. But it wasn't and she hadn't been.

Cade had been sixteen when she'd been arrested for shoplifting. It was lift or starve and she thought that she could get out faster than the clerk could. She might have, too, if the cop, Gabriel Sheets, hadn't walked in when he had. He'd tackled her with all his weight and had nearly broken her arm in the process. As it was she'd had three broken ribs for her problems. When he refused to get her medical treatment the shop owner had threatened to call Gabriel's boss. She got her treatment, but it did her little good when she couldn't afford the pain pills or the food to take them with. Gabriel had taken her to the station anyway, even after he was told no charges would be pressed against her.

"You are one lucky bitch, you know that? Any other cop would have taken a piece of your ass by now, but you got me. What do you think of that?"

She had since learned to curb her mouth, but back then she said whatever popped into her mind. "What? You couldn't get your dick up so I'm supposed to be grateful? Sorry, but you don't impress me with your humanitarian ways when you're the one who beat the shit out of me in the first place."

The slap knocked her off the chair. She nearly lost conciseness, too, when she banged her ribs against the table leg. When she sat up again and blood poured from her upper lip she spit at him. That got her another slap; this one did take her out. When she woke up she was sitting in a jail cell and her hands were cuffed behind her.

"You behave yourself, kid, and I'll let you live. One less punk on the streets is fine by me. I don't care one way or the other. And if you tell that brother of yours what happened here I'll make your life a living hell."

Cade started to say he'd been doing a bang up job of that already, but decided that she'd probably live longer if she didn't. Her body hurt and the thought of leaving with Garrett didn't sound any better than being in the cell. That's when she noticed the computer on the floor in front of him and Garrett at the desk asleep with his feet up on the desk.

"Yeah, your brother and I have had a nice long chat about you. Seems you could be useful to me alive rather than dead. He was telling me about this nice little thing you can do with accounts. I think I might like to see you do that."

The laptop slid over toward her. She didn't know how he thought she was going to use it with her hands behind her back, but she kept her mouth shut. Cade didn't even look at it as it slid within a foot of her feet.

"You're going to use that little talent of yours to break into this account for me and move the funds to mine. If you're good then I'll let you go when you're finished. Otherwise, you'll be hanging out with me for a bit longer. Here's the account numbers and the amount I want you to move. If you fuck this up you'll be the one going to prison, not me. Stand up and put your back to the cell walls here and I'll let you go. Don't fuck with me on this, kid, or else."

"Or else what? I'm already in jail. What the fuck else can you do to me? Kill me? If I keep going the way I am I'll be dead in no time anyway. Rape me? Sure, you do that and I'll give you the itchy diseases that I have already. Matters little to me."

Gabriel looked over at her brother. Garrett had meant little to her since her mom had married Cade's stepfather five years ago. Garrett was older than her by six years and acted like he was ten most of the time. He had also been mean. Not as mean as he was now; he'd gotten stronger with age, but mean. If he threatened her with killing him she might have him pop some popcorn so she could enjoy it while she watched.

Cade couldn't defend herself against Garrett. His father had beaten her every time she'd tried. Then when telling on him to the authorities had gotten her nowhere, she'd just simply avoided him at all costs. Her mother was no help. She had been drinking heavily before she'd married Daniel Reid and now she drank more. Cade would never have thought that even possible.

"I know you don't care for him. He told me as much. But you do care for the lady next door, Mrs. Ida Marsh, and her grandchild, Chesney. What if I told you that if you don't help me I'll kill them both? I will. And I'll never get caught either. Will you help me?"

"Fuck off. I'm not helping you do anything. If you don't let me go I'm going to start screaming for someone to come help me. I'm sick of you and your shit."

Cade didn't know what to think when he stood up, came to the cell door, and opened it. She thought for sure that he was going to hit her again and cowered down on the cell's only bed. But he had simply flipped her over and uncuffed her. When he stepped back to let her go she almost didn't move. She thought he'd just shoot her in the back as she did. As she moved toward the door to leave the station house she kept looking and waiting for someone to come and get her or to take her back inside.

But nothing happened. Nothing happened then at any rate.

The sirens woke her up the next morning. It wasn't as if she never heard them on her street, but they were very close and not moving on like they normally did. It took her a few moments to realize that they had stopped next door. Cade rushed out the door when the ambulance pulled up in front of the little house. Cade was standing there waiting with the rest of the neighborhood when her step-brother and Gabriel walked up to her. Her body froze when they started talking.

"Shoulda helped him, Cade. Shame a couple of nice people had to die 'cause you're a stubborn bitch. Yeah, terrible shame. Tell her, Gabe. Tell her what happened next door."

"Someone just broke in and killed both those nice people. Killed the little baby first while the old woman watched, I was told. Seems Mrs. Marsh was told that it was because of you that poor little Chesney was dead. Your brother is right, you should have helped me. Now I'm going to give you another—"

Cade had attacked him. It didn't do her much good. Her broken ribs and small body was no match for the big man. Then when he'd thrown her to the ground her step-brother had kicked her. She'd slipped into unconsciousness within seconds.

When Cade had woken up in the hospital there was a laptop sitting on the little table and a sticky note with two numbers on it. When she'd opened the lid on the computer there was a picture of the couple down the street from her family and their little boy. The red line through their faces made her open the Internet connection and do what she had to do. That had been ten years ago.

The first five, she'd done just what he told her to do. Every time she would get her envelope from him there would be a new picture. She'd only told him no once more and when three people she'd worked with had been murdered and their shop burned to the ground she'd never argued again. But she did plan. Plan and save to leave the area and start a new life. That's how she had ended up in Ohio. But six months ago her brother Garrett had found her again. And with him he'd brought Gabriel.

Taking a deep breath and releasing it slowly Cade connected to the Internet and opened the program to the bank accounts. With trembling hands she reached for the mouse and as soon as she made a connection to it she felt whatever it was that happened tingle through her body. It only took Cade eleven minutes to complete the transaction and three more to move the money. She was closing down the computer twenty minutes after she first keyed in. Cade had just stolen one point seven million dollars out of someone's account and transferred it to one far across the world into another.

Cade was wandering the streets a few hours later. She felt someone following her and it didn't register until the person was nearly on top of her. At this point she couldn't fight them, didn't even know if she wanted to. Her strength was drained from whatever it was she used up to make the computer work for her and when the black sedan pulled up beside her and her step-brother got out she didn't even stop walking.

"I need that money, Cade. Where is it? This guy wants it now. I told him that you'd need a couple of days to get it together, but he doesn't want to wait. For some reason he doesn't trust me."

"Go figure. Did you tell him I don't trust you either? It doesn't matter. I don't have it. I told you the other day I didn't have it and I don't know why you think the situation has changed. You are going to have to get your money the old fashioned way, work for it."

Cade braced herself for the hit or whatever else it was. When he threw her against the wall and knocked the wind out of her, she didn't even fight him. In fact, Cade had no idea where she even was or how he'd found her in the first place. Before she could ask, he started slapping her. After the fourth hit she just stopped counting. But at some point she realized she was alone. Garrett was gone.

"You need a keeper, has anyone ever told you that before? My name is Daniel Taggert. I work for Aaron. Can you stand or do you need help up?"

"I'm fine, thanks. Let me go. Where's...you'd better leave before Garrett gets back. He doesn't much like his beating time interrupted."

The giggle escaped before she could sensor it. The man standing over her looked at her oddly, but didn't say anything. Suddenly, she was standing upright and then she was in his arms. She tried to pull away from him, but he growled at her. Growled? Oh well, things are certainly getting more Wonderland-like every day, she thought.

"Are you talking to yourself or are you talking to me? Shawn said you were a little overwhelmed by all this. The man who was hitting you when I came up? That guy was your boyfriend? He took off when he saw me coming at him. I wished he'd hung around. I had to see to you or I'd have given chase. He might have been fun to chew on for a bit."

"Maybe next time you can. And not my boyfriend, I don't have one of those. He's my step-brother. Do you think you could put me down? I think I'm going to be really sick and I don't want to throw up all over you. I think I might have a concussion. It's been a very strange day."

Daniel stopped immediately and put her down. She barely made it to the ground before she started throwing up. Cade couldn't remember the last time she ate or what she'd eaten. She tried to think about it, but it was just too hard. When her belly was empty and the heaving stopped she just sat there for several minutes resting.

"You okay? If you promise to stay right here I'll go inside here and get you a cola. But if I have to come and find you again I may have to beat your...never mind. Just stay here until I return."

Cade thought about telling him she didn't have the energy to move much less get up and walk again. She closed her eyes and thought about what he'd said. Aaron MacManus. This man said that he worked for Aaron. And Shawn said she was overwhelmed. Well, damn it, it had been a lot, but these two men were going to get a piece of her mind when she found them again. When Daniel came back with not only a cola but a bag of chips she didn't know whether to kiss him or kick him. She decided to wait on both until she felt better.

"You look better, though I'm going to take you to the clinic to make sure. Shawn said that I was to watch over you and make sure you were safe. I had a hard time finding you after you left the mansion or you're step-brother wouldn't have hurt you. What did you say his name was again?"

"I didn't. And I'm not going to any clinic. I appreciate you running him off, but I'm fine now. I've got a lot of stuff to do today before I have to be at work tonight. So why don't you go away?"

Daniel just smiled at her. He was sitting on the ground in front of her and she wanted to smack him. Arrogant dickhead, she thought. She decided to ignore him and continue with her day. She hurt and was sure her face was really bloody, but she really did have things to do. When his cell phone went off, she stood up and started walking back the way she'd come. When he pecked her on the shoulder and handed her his cell she took it.

"Go to the clinic. Why do you have to be so—"

Cade closed the phone on Shawn and handed it back to Daniel. She didn't even look back at him as she continued on. When Daniel's phone rang he handed it to her.

"I'm going to assume that we had a bad connection and that you didn't just hang up on me. Damn it, Cade, why don't you just do what you're—"

This time, before she handed him back the phone she turned it off first.

"You're really going to piss him off like that. While I don't really care for myself, it's you who is going to pay when the sun goes down and he gets to you. I haven't known him long, but the little I have known him I would say he has a protective streak when it comes to you."

"I can't imagine why. I have to get to work, Mr. Taggert. You should really move along. I don't like Mr.

MacFarland very much right now and myself even less. Goodbye."

Cade suddenly found herself lying on the sidewalk. While she'd been talking to Daniel she'd heard a car coming, but had no idea why it would register to her. Then when she was laying face-down on the sidewalk with Daniel on top of her, it took her several seconds to realize there were bullets flying over their heads.

"Someone is shooting? I don't believe it. Let me see if I can—"

"Will you stay the fuck down? Christ, that man is tenacious. You're going to have to tell me his name now. He just fucking shot me."

CHAPTER 10

Cade was still lying on the hospital bed when Shawn threw the curtain back. She'd opened her mouth and he was sure she was either going to blast him or scream, so he covered it with his hand. His heart was still pounding and had been since he'd felt her terror.

"I'm going to take my hand away and you're going to be quiet. If you so much as open your mouth to yawn I may be driven to strangle you. Why I ever let you out of my sight is beyond me. What has the doctor said about your injuries?"

He removed his hand and stepped back to look at her. When she just sat there staring at him he cocked a brow. Damned woman was going to drive him nuts.

"I asked you a question, Cade. I would suggest that you behave yourself and answer me. I'm in no mood to play your little power games that you're just going to lose anyway."

Still nothing. With a deep growl he left her to find the doctor, anyone to keep him from screaming at her. She was hurt and bleeding and he wanted to throw her over his shoulder, take her home, and heal her. He also wanted to go and find the bastard who hurt her. Shawn was nearly to the front desk when he realized why she wasn't speaking. He'd told her not to. Of all the times for her to listen, now was not the time. He nearly stormed back in behind the curtain when he heard her crying. That did him in faster than her wounds.

"I'm sorry, baby. Please don't cry, Cade. Please? Here, let me hold you. Stop fighting me, I'm stronger and bigger."

"You're a bully. Let me go. I have to pee. There was no reason for them to shoot poor Mr. Taggert. He was only there because you guys won't leave me the hell alone. I told you to leave me to myself. But oh no, you have to be all big and macho. I was doing all right before—"

Shawn couldn't stand it anymore. He pulled her into his arms and crushed her to him. She was all right, cranky, but all right. He wanted to kiss her, wanted to pull that luscious body of hers up to his and take her. Take her right then and there on the stupid bed where anyone could come in and see. His need to mark her again was weighing heavily on his body, heart, and mind.

Moving his mouth down along the column of her neck he closed his eyes when she responded to his nearness. Her scent crushed him with need. Licking the pounding pulse it was everything he could do not to bite her. When she whimpered he ran his fangs along the vein; not breaking the skin, but coming very close.

"I want to taste you again. Sink my fangs deep into you and drink from you. You're like a drug and I can't get enough of you, Cade. I can't think when your body is close to mine. I can't breathe when you're this close to me, not when I can feel your heat, smell your arousal. I bet if I were to run my hand up under this gown I'd find you soaking, drenching wet. Oh, Cade."

Her legs parted for him when he ran his hand up her thigh. His cock jerked hard in his pants and he thought if she touched him now he'd come immediately. When his fingers ran along the band at her leg just under the tiny material he felt her muscles quiver under his fingers. Pulling the shadows around them quickly he slid his fingers under the band and into her slit. He captured her moan with his mouth. Moving along her throat again, he licked the pulse as he fucked her with his fingers.

"Cade, come for me, baby. Come and let me mark you, taste you. Christ, baby, you're so hot that I can't wait to bury my cock deep within you."

As soon as she arched up and began riding his fingers as she clung to him, he licked her pulse again and sank into her vein. He couldn't take much; he wasn't hungry. But he did need to mark her. The need to mark her as his became harder and harder to stop. When she came this time, hard and quick, he nearly came with her. Her pussy spasmed and tightened around him, milked his fingers like he knew she would his cock if he were to strip down and slam into her deep.

When her hand cupped against his cock through his pants then worked at his zipper, he nearly came then. When she had his cock free of his jeans but still hidden behind his briefs he heard her growl at him or his pants, he wasn't quite sure. Sealing the wounds at her throat he shifted and helped her free his cock. Her hand was hot against it. And when she took the drop of pre-cum off the tip into her mouth he nearly threw her to her back and fucked her then.

"I want to taste you, but my mouth...I don't think I can do it without hurting...Shawn, can you come for me, come hard and let me taste you this way?"

She wanted him to come, wanted him to bring himself to climax so that she could lick him clean. Taking her hand into his he rubbed it up and down his shaft. With his fingers he showed her how to pleasure him, how he liked to be touched, caressed, and squeezed. Soon he was leaning back on his hands while she encircled him, while she pulled and tugged on his cock until he knew he was so close, almost too close to let her continue without coming.

"I can come on you like this or inside of you. I'm so close, baby, that either way is going to be fast. Come sit on my cock and ride me. I want to feel you come again."

When Cade started to rise up he lifted her and settled her across his lap even as he turned more onto the bed. When her panties got in the way he reached down between them and cut them from her body with a sharp claw. She settled her pussy over him and dropped down. He came. As soon as she was seated over him he shot his seed deep into her womb. Over and over his cock surged and filled her and when she came with him, hers mere seconds behind his, he felt his cock surge again. As if he was having a second climax.

Cade was asleep when he laid her back on the bed. He pulled her clothes over her then covered her with the thin blanket. Straightening his own clothes he dropped the shadows and reached out beyond the little area where they were. Aaron was close. Reaching out to his friend he asked him to keep everyone away for a little while longer.

"Is she all right? Daniel is in surgery to remove the bullet, but as soon as he shifts he'll be fine. I'm not sure what we would have done if the EMT hadn't realized that Daniel was a were and brought him here to the clinic."

Shawn wasn't sure either. He knew that weres would return to their human state once they were injured or lost consciousness, but he had no idea what happened when they were hurt and still in human form. He'd have to ask Bradley the next time he saw him.

"She's fine. For now at any rate. I can't say what will happen when she wakes up and I have to strangle her. She is the most stubborn woman I've ever met. But Aaron, I've never been so scared in my entire lifetime as I was when I felt her terror at being shot at. Have you heard anything?"

"No. Not a thing. Daniel was already in surgery by the time I had the thought to ask to see him. Sara is beside herself with worry and has surrounded Cade in protection. Sara is very strong, so Cade'll be safe. At least for now at any rate. We've no idea what or who we're dealing with or why they want her dead. Were you able to get anything from her before she...ah, well, that works too. I find Sara to be much easier to talk to when she's completely sated."

Shawn flushed. Damned man was inside of his mind again. Shawn turned to look at the beautiful woman on the bed. She was bruised again. Her lip was cut and her cheeks were both swollen. He wanted to make her drink from him, but knew that this time if he healed her she'd know. He needed to get her mated to him. Reaching down to run his fingers over her cheek he remembered something. He reached for Aaron again.

"Aaron, the reason I was coming here. I needed your advice on becoming a master. I was going to challenge Mason for his realm and wanted to get the correct rules governing the challenge."

"I see. You should have been given those when you made your intentions known to the current master. Did you? Let him know, I mean? If you did then that could explain why you were ambushed. He wanted to take you out before the challenge."

Shawn wasn't surprised that Aaron knew this. He was one of the smartest men he knew. There was a wealth of information inside Aaron's head and Shawn was willing to bet that if given the time, he'd be able to tell Shawn every person he'd meet since he'd been changed.

"Maybe. I don't know. The woman, Pete, was she able to find out anything on Dana? I know that she is key for some reason. She knew something was going to happen, but for some reason I don't think she was really a part of it."

"Pete called right after we got the call about Daniel. I'll call her back now and get back with you. Shawn, I know that you are aware of this, but you need to bond and mate with Cade. She's in danger. I don't want to make you do it, but she's your mate and you need to claim her. She'll be able to handle much more if she has your strength added to her own."

Shawn knew he was right, but he didn't want to force her to make that decision. But looking at her now he realized that if Daniel hadn't come along when he had she'd be dead. And if she had had his blood in her system, the full bond and mate, then she would already be healed. It was time, past time, and he knew it.

"I'll talk to her when we get back to the lair. She's hurt again and I'm reluctant to heal her for fear of pissing her off more than I've already done by making love with her. Aaron, do you suppose there will be a time when she isn't pissed at me?"

"I hope not. It's so much more fun to have a passionate mate than one that lets you get by with much. Fighting with your mate is far much more challenging than any war I've ever fought in, more exciting than any new discovery I've come across over the centuries, and much, much more fun to make up with than anyone I've ever met. Learn to enjoy it. It'll be much more fun that way."

Shawn closed the connection between them. There was always an open line, so to speak. They had exchanged blood often through the years for one thing or another, so they had a bond that would never be broken. But neither man would cross the boundaries of privacy without a dire need.

~~~

Cade woke to the bright sunshine and people in her room she didn't know. Sara was there and so were four other women. They were all arguing about the state of being...of being a unicorn verses a horse?

"I did so tell you. I've told you three hundred times and you know it. Why I even bother is beyond me. I swear I'm going to get you one of those little note pads and put it on a chain and attach it to your neck. Cornwall is not a male, but a female. And when she finds a mate she said she's naming the first colt Banquo."

"What a horrible name. Why, I ask you? Why doesn't she name it Pinkeye or some other ridiculous name like that? Some people shouldn't be allowed to breed. Of all the things in the world to do."

"It's the name of the ghost, a character in Shakespeare's play Macbeth." Cade said and had them turning as one toward her. "The ghost of Banquo appears to Macbeth, who had ordered his murder. Who are you people? And why on earth do you care about a baby named after a mythical ghost in a Shakespearian play written in the sixteen hundreds? Or do I even what to know?"

Cade was startled when they turned and looked at her. They were beautiful. Breathtakingly, drop-dead, holy crap beautiful. They smiled at her and Cade knew that they had been listening in her mind. She pushed back. Not hard, but enough to make them realize that they had not been invited. It was easier than she thought it'd be.

"Yes, that's because we let you. My, but you are a pretty little thing, aren't you? My name is Elizabeth. This is my daughter Savannah and her daughter Melody. You know Sara, and this is our friend Shade. How are you, dear?"

"Fine. Where is...do you think I can have my clothes? I think I'd very much like to go now." And go she would. She didn't know where Shawn was, but figured that with him out of the room she'd just leave now and keep him safe. Gabriel wasn't balanced and she was not going to have any more deaths on her head.

"I'm afraid you won't be able to hide now, Cade. Shawn has your blood. It's like a beacon to him. He'll be able to find you no matter where you are. Why don't you tell us about this Gabriel person? She sounds like where we need to start," Sara said.

"Stay out of my head. Gabriel is a he, not a she. And I won't be telling you...why on earth would he want to find me anyway? Oh yeah, the food thing. There has to be a way for him to get something to eat from somebody else. I'm not exactly approved by the FDA or anything."

The women laughed. Cade glared at them. She started to move from the bed when she felt a stirring. An unpleasant something...someone was near. Her step-brother. Before she could warn the women both Shade and Sara stood up and turned toward the door. Elizabeth came to stand next to Cade and the other two women merely sat where they were.

"He'll not harm you, Cade. Not while I'm here. Especially not now. Let him come in. I swear to you he'll not be able to harm you."

Cade couldn't tell who had spoken until she looked at the one they'd called Melody. When the woman winked at Cade she knew for sure that it had been her. She was about to ask her what she meant when the door opened and her step-brother walked in.

"Caddy. Who are these people and why the fuck are they here? This is a private room and that's what it should be, private."

Garrett stared at her as if she would suddenly shoo the women out of her room just because he said so. She just looked at him. She hadn't realized she was in a private room until he said so and she also knew that he wasn't paying for it so he didn't get to decide who stayed or not.

"Did you hear me? I said to kick these women out. I have some things to tell you and they are better said in private."

"Go to hell, Garrett. And you did not tell me to kick them out. You asked me who they were, you dumb fuck. I'm sick of you ordering me around. I would very much like it if you left me alone. Not only in this room, but in my life."

When he lunged toward her Shade stepped in front of him. Cade didn't know where the long knife she had in her hand had come from, but it was suddenly at Garrett's throat. He didn't move. Shade took a step toward him and he backed up. They did this little dance three more times until he was back near the door.

"She told you to leave. I believe that you should, don't you? You should also know that I don't mind killing you. I've killed before and will gladly kill you as well. Leave before you piss me off anymore." Shade's voice was low, but there was steel in it that was stronger than the blade she held at Garrett's throat. When he started forward again Shade dipped the blade into his skin and drew blood. His anger was palatable. Garrett looked as though he would gladly kill Shade as well.

"I'll talk to you later, Caddy. I want that money. All of it. You'll get it for me or else. I'm tired of fucking with you about it. Either get the money or I'll make you get it for me. You owe me." Then he was gone.

Cade looked at the women in the room. She could feel it now, magic she supposed. And lots of it. These people weren't like anything or anyone she'd ever met before. When she started to ask Elizabeth started talking.

"You aren't human, my dear. Not all human anyway. There are things you should know before you meet up with that horrid man again."

CHAPTER 11

Aaron watched the girl sleep. He'd been told by Sara what had happened today and what Mel and the others had told her about her birth and what she was. Sara said that Cade had not said much, but she knew that Cade was going to need answers about what she was later. That's why he was waiting for her to wake. When she opened her eyes and stared at him he waited for her to speak first.

"I'm part vampire, they said. That woman Eliz said that my father was a vampire and that my mother, my real mother, was a faerie. She didn't know how I ended up with those people, but she said she could maybe find out. She said she'd even find my parents or find out if both of them were dead."

Aaron let her talk. He knew that she had questions, he could practically feel them brimming around in her head. But she calmly told him what she knew. He let her even though he had been told yesterday before Eliz and the others had come to tell Cade what she was. "I'm sorry for your loss, Cade. I'm sorry more that you never knew your parents. Is there anything I can answer for you?"

"I know that this is stupid, but I don't suppose you know my father? I don't know if there are lots of your kind out there, or if you have some sort of...I don't know. I was going to say connection, but I'm not sure that's what I meant either."

"I knew of your father. I'd never met him, but I'd heard stories about him. Sara said his name was Vladimir Michaels. He's very old and very powerful. I have someone searching for him now. I don't know yet if he's alive. He was a born vampire rather than a made one, like me. His family was part of the first vampires ever known. The reason I never felt your connection is because your Faerie mother had put a protection about you. Mel was able to break it down and figure out the magic and then the signature of the person who made it. Mel will have more information later, I'm told. She said to tell you that she knows who your mother was and has her things for you. I'm not sure what that entails, but she'll explain."

"What happens now? I mean, I don't have...I'm not sure what I'm supposed to do with this information. Mrs. MacManus...Sara showed me some things. Will I now burn up in the sun? I'm so...what do I do now?"

"The information tells you what you are, Cade, it doesn't define you. The protection kept you from changing when you needed to. According to Mel's grandmother you'll be able to shift now and whatever magic you had before, it'll be stronger now. And more varied. The sun won't bother you because you are only part vamp. You can drink blood if you want or not."

She didn't say anything, but stared into the room. Aaron felt Shawn coming near them. Aaron had asked him to come now. His memory was coming back in leaps and bounds, but the reason he'd been attacked at the bar still eluded him.

"I can feel Shawn coming. He's very close. I think...he's at the nurses' station. What will he think when he finds out, Mr. MacManus?"

"He'll be fine with it, Cade. I'd like for you to call me Aaron. You are now a part of my Kiss and as such will need to learn the rules of the realm. I'm now your master until you find one that you'd like to pledge to. Shawn will be able to tell you all that that entails. I'm going to go now. Someday soon you will pledge yourself to me or someone like me. Until then you may reach me at anytime. Cade, as a member of my Kiss I will protect you. It is my duty to do so whether you want it or not. It will be a broken law of my kind if I don't."

Cade didn't say anything. When Shawn opened the door he had a dozen red roses and a box of candy in his hands. Aaron might have laughed at any other time, but didn't. He thought about stopping on his way back to the mansion to pick up some flowers for Sara. And maybe a nice little outfit that he could tear from her body. He felt his cock harden at the thought and shimmered from the room with a nod to Shawn.

~~~

Shawn laid the flowers on the table and the chocolate next to it. He could feel Cade's emotions. They were strong and varied. Mostly she was confused. He couldn't blame her for that. In the two weeks since he'd met her she'd been through a great deal. He didn't say anything, but slipped off his shoes and his shirt. He was taking off his pants when she turned to look at him. He thought he'd have to argue with her, but she simply rolled back over and moved more to the edge of the bed. He left his boxers on, slid into the bed behind her, and spooned against her.

"I don't have a job anymore. Paul called me today and told me that he was really sorry, but I'd missed too much work and he'd had to replace me. He still wants me to be his friend. I haven't worked for the MacManuses much either so I don't have that job either, I guess. Penny will be returning on Monday now so I guess it doesn't matter."

Shawn almost told her that she didn't need to work, that he would take care of her, but simply kissed her shoulder. He pulled her body close to his and held her as she continued to speak.

"Mel said that I'm part vampire. I don't have a sudden carving for blood, but she said that was okay. Aaron said my father was a pureblood, a born vampire. I didn't know there was such a thing. What are you?"

"Turned. My maker thought I'd make a great addition to her bedroom. Purebloods are rare. I know that Tristan, another of the Kiss, is one as are his other family members."

"You told me that before. I'm sorry. I guess...it's been very strange these past few days. I have to tell you something. I...it's about my step-brother—well, I guess he's not my step-brother anymore. But there's something you should know. He's...that's to say I think...Shawn, do you think we could have sex? I really need it right now. I know that I have a lot to tell you, but right now, I need you."

Shawn leaned back as she rolled to her back. She'd been crying. Her cheeks were wet from her tears and her eyes were reddened. In that moment he knew that he was in love with her. Pulling her closer, he gently brushed his mouth over hers.

"I'd rather make love to you, Cade. I think we've been having sex before, but now I'd rather make love with you. And I need you right now as well. Whatever you have to tell me can wait. We have through eternity to tell each other."

Cade nodded. With trembling hands she reached up and unsnapped the buttons at her shoulders. She didn't pull the material away, but rolled more until she was facing him. Looking deep into his eyes she put her hand over his heart.

"I don't know what to do to bond with you. Will you show me? That's if you still want me."

"Yes. I want you more than anything in this world. Are you sure, Cade? Once we go through with this, you're mine and I am yours. We will be a mated couple for all eternity. Our lives will change when we exchange blood. You'll be able to do whatever I can do and I will do what you can do."

"Yes. I'm sure. Sara explained it to me today. She said that we'd have to...that we'd have to exchange blood during a climax and that it would be incredible. I'm ready."

Shawn felt his heart pounding through his head. The roaring had gotten louder with her every word and when she'd said she was ready Shawn wanted to shout from the highest mountains tops. He rolled to his back and pulled her over him.

"When we make love this time I won't bite until we are both ready to come. Then once we are coming I'll bite your wrist while you drink from a wound on my chest. I'll make the cut and you'll take my blood there. The climax will be intense, but you can't stop sipping until we are both completely finished. Once we are finished, then you can seal the wound I make with your tongue. Cade, I'm not going to last long. The thought of you having your mouth over me has me harder than stone. I want to bury myself deep inside of you. Are you ready?"

"Yes. But I...I figured out how to make them work. Well, I didn't. Sara told me how to think about them, how to want them there and I felt them pulse in my mouth. All I could think about was sinking them into you like you did me. I don't know if I can do it or not, but I'd like to...will you let me try to bite you first."

Shawn's cock hurt. It felt as if she'd poured hot lava over it and then she'd licked him dry. When he'd told her he was close he never anticipated her biting him.

"Show me. Show me your fangs, love." When she opened her mouth and they elongated he had to close his eyes and count to ten. She looked worried when he opened them. She was looking at him. "That's probably the most beautiful sight I've ever seen. I want you to lick my pulse like I do before I feed from you. Lick the area with your tongue and when I tell you to, bite me. Bite me like you did my nipple that first day. When you break the skin there my blood will fill your mouth. Drink from me, Cade. Suckle at my vein and join me."

They both seemed to recognize that their lovemaking wasn't going to last. He moved to pull the gown away from her breast and took the hard nipple into his mouth as he rolled her to her back. She immediately wrapped her legs around his hips and surged up into him. Reaching down to cup her ass while he moved along her ribs with his mouth, he was happy to feel that she had not replaced her panties. When her hands grabbed at his boxers he moved his hand to the front of them and ripped them from his hips. She giggled at him.

"If I didn't want to ram my cock deep into you this very second I'd roll you over and beat your ass for that. Never giggle in bed with a vamp. It could be very painful to sit for a few days."

Shawn's voice was gruff, but she smiled at him and rocked up again. This time, his cock slid into her several inches. When he pressed down he groaned, when he was fully seated inside of her. When she moved again, pulling him deeper, he growled at her.

"Don't...Christ, I want to slam into you hard and take you, but don't move. I'm not going to last much longer. I love you, Cade. I'm going to spend the rest of my life making you happy."

"Then do you think you could start right now and make me come? Please, I want to feel you come deep...yes!"

He moved hard into her, pulled out to near the tip, and rocked again. As he slammed back into her he nuzzled her neck. When she moved her mouth over his throat he tilted his head to allow her whatever room she needed. Her tongue felt like a torch across his skin. Pulling out again, he moved slowly into her this time and felt her body pull then tighten around him. When she clamped tight enough around him to bring him to peak he licked her pulse. Feeling her do the same sent him over the edge.

"Now, baby, bite now." As her teeth broke the skin he did the same to her. Ecstasy! Her rich, hot blood filled him like never before. As she drew against his vein he pumped into her hard. Over and over as his seed filled her, she pulled and milked him both at his cock and at his throat, her grip on his cock hard and tight. When she went limp beneath him, still suckling at his vein, he rocked again. Then again until he was complete, his body sated. When he licked the wound at her throat closed, Cade did the same and he dropped over her. He knew he was heavy and was probably crushing her, but short of a fire there was no way he was moving from her.

When he finally rolled to his back on the narrow bed he pulled her with him. Shawn was still deep within her, his cock semi-hard and pulsing again. When she lifted her head and rested her chin on his chest he looked down at her.

"What happens now? Are we finished? Do I belong to you? I'm sorry. You must think I'm terribly stupid and naive."

"No. I don't think that. Are we finished? Not by a long shot. We are only just starting. And yes, you belong to me as much as I belong to you. We are a mated couple, a pair. Vampires go for centuries looking for their mate. Some give up like I had. I never thought I'd find you. And now that I have I can't let you go. I'm not sure what the future will bring. I still have a lot of memory loss that I feel I need to figure out before I feel safe enough for us to travel back to my home."

Shawn rolled her to her back and followed. His cock was hard now and he rocked into her heat. When her legs wrapped around him he looked down into her eyes. "You're healed now. I want very much to kiss you, taste you. I don't think I'll ever get enough of you. I want to take you home, make love to you in a proper bed, not this tiny thing we're in where I can't move the way I want. Will you stay with me now, Cade? All I have to offer you is a place in Aaron's home. But we'll take care of that soon."

"I'll go where you go. I don't think...I'm not sure I could be anywhere that you're not. Are you going to make love to me again now? I'd very much like that. It's a wonderful feeling having you deep inside of me."

He never got a chance to answer her. A knock at the door prevented it. He did shout at whoever was at the door to go away, making Cade giggle again. With a swift kiss to her mouth and another shout at the door he stood to get dressed. He had to stop several times when he forgot what he was doing, just watching her.

"You wait. When I get you home you're not leaving the lair until I'm totally sated. And that could be a very long time." Her growl made his cock twitch and the need to strip down again was overwhelming.

Shawn had never felt this way before. Light, buoyant, and free. He wanted to shout to the world that he'd found his mate and he wanted to hide her away from the others and keep her all to himself. When he was dressed he went to the door and unlocked it. Thomas Reilly came blustering in.

"I'm going to have those locks removed as soon as I can. I swear there are more people getting laid in this clinic than there are in most human homes. Hello, my dear, how are you feeling tonight?"

With a glare at Shawn, Thomas set to work. It took several tense minutes to assure Thomas that he wasn't leaving. Shawn seemed to think that as her mate it was his right and Thomas thought that since he was the doctor and the one in charge he had the same rights. Shawn, being older and much stronger both physically and magically, won. Cade simply watched them and when Shawn sat on the bed next to her, she had the nerve to smack him. Ungrateful wench, she was going to pay for that. His excitement built as Thomas finished up his exam. When Thomas declared her well and released her Shawn called Aaron for a ride home.

CHAPTER 12

Cade woke to a dark room. She could feel Shawn lying next to her and started to snuggle up next to him, but realized that she had to go to the bathroom. Getting up, she realized she was naked. Again. Picking up the shirt that Shawn had had on when they came here she smiled, went to the bath, and closed the door.

Flipping on the light she took a look at herself. She didn't look any different. Her skin wasn't marked anymore. The bruises that Garrett had given her were completely gone. Opening her mouth she willed her fangs to show.

It was very odd to see them come in. They dropped from her gums just above her eye teeth. It didn't hurt. On the contrary, they felt sort of nice, sexy. When she thought about biting Shawn, they actually got longer and thicker. Running her finger over the point she was surprised at how sharp they were. Moving back from the mirror she removed his shirt.

Her body didn't look any different either. She turned to her left and then to her right to examine herself and that's when she found the mark. It wasn't very big, but it was bright. Sitting up on the counter after not being able to find a little mirror, she looked at it. It was a small faerie.

The faerie was golden, its hair, clothes, and shoes. The wings at her back were long, reaching from the top of her head to just to her knees. In her hands were flowers, golden and yellow-colored ones. The fairie's eyes were dark blue like Cade's were. When Cade put her hand over the tattoo she could feel the heat emanating from it. Deciding to keep this little bit of news to herself, Cade took a shower. Her clothes were hanging in the closet, what little she had. Grabbing the first things she touched, she pulled them on, walked over to the big bed, and kissed the man lying there.

Cade knew that Shawn had to sleep during the highest point of the day. He'd told her last night that she wasn't to leave the mansion until he could go with her. She knew that he had her personal wellbeing in mind so she had full intentions of listening to him. That was until she got to the kitchen and Duncan told her that Paul had called.

"Cade, he has my daughter. He has Daisy. He said that if you didn't call him back that he'd kill her and that it would be your fault. I don't know how he got her. Her room is on the third floor and her windows where all locked up. Please tell me you'll call him back. Please, I need my little girl."

"I'll call him right now, Paul. I'm so sorry. I never thought to have him...I'll call him right now. I'll call you back when I've talked to him. I'm so sorry, Paul."

After she hung up the phone she felt someone touch her mind, then speak softly to her. It was Shawn. He'd felt her emotions through their connection.

"Are you all right, love? I can feel your anger and your sorrow. Come back to bed and let me hold you. Then whatever it is, we'll work it out together."

"I'm fine. Really. I'm just nervous. I've never been...I was nervous that I'd burn up in the sun is all. I'm fine now. Rest. I need you to be at full strength for tonight. I plan to take your cock deep into my mouth and have you come down my throat."

"If you come back to bed now, I might let you do that to me now. Christ, my cock is hard. Come here, Cade. I need you."

"I have to get online and order me some clothes. I have nothing to wear in public. And as much as I love being naked with you I can't spend my days and nights in that state of undress. What would the household think if I did?"

"Fuck them. But I can see your point. All right, but I expect to see your naked body right here next to me when I rise. I can't wait to feel you take me into your mouth."

He sent her images of them from last night. Need rippled over her body and made her almost want to just go to him and tell him everything. But she couldn't. She'd hoped that Gabriel would have finished with her by now but she was wrong. She knew that the last move she'd made for him had been well over ten million dollars. And that was only less than a week ago. Trying hard not to cry Cade asked Duncan if there was a phone she could make a private call on.

"It's Cade. If you want my help then you'll take Daisy back to her parents right now. When I have proof that she's home and fine I'll do this one last move for you."

"Oh? And since when do you make the rules? You'll do as I tell you when I tell you and nothing more. I fucking own you, you stupid bitch. You think that you can—"

She hung up. It was risky, she knew. For one thing, he didn't have any way to call her back. For another, she wasn't sure that little Daisy wasn't already dead. Watching the minute hand move slowly around the face, she waited five full minutes before she called him back.

"You take her back and I'll work this last job. Otherwise you'll have to deal with me. I'm not the same kid I was when you made me start this. I make the rules now." Cade concentrated on her breathing as she spoke. She also tried to keep her heart from pounding out of her chest. She tightened the hold on her mind and reinforced her walls. Keeping Shawn safe was more important than anything.

"You'll regret this, you fucking cunt. When this is over, you'll pay. You'll pay in ways you never dreamed of."

Ten minutes later Duncan let her know that she had a phone call. She had just hung up from talking with the alpha of the wolf pack. Picking up the extension she was relieved to hear Paul's voice. Daisy was home.

"Paul, there's a man coming to you. His name is Bradley Wolff. Go with him. The man who took Daisy might come back and I need to make sure you're safe. Bradley will make sure that you are safe for me."

Cade hoped so anyway. She had taken a chance calling the alpha. When the person who'd answered the phone had asked who she was she'd told him she was the mate of Shawn MacFarland and that she needed to leave a message for the alpha. He'd come on the phone almost immediately.

"Hello, Cade. My mate and I were just talking about you. Congratulations on your being newly mated. I've met Shawn. He's a good man. What can I do for you?"

It took her five minutes to give him a very brief idea of what was going on. He had asked only one question and that had been where her mate was.

"He's asleep. I can't cause him harm and I can't...please do this for me. I promise I'll explain as soon as I can. He has a hold over me that Shawn may...I'm not a good person, Mr. Wolff."

"I'll do this for you. But you will explain. And in great detail. I understand the urgency for now. Tell Paul that I'll come for him now. I should be there in ten minutes. I have a crew that I've already sent to the home. As soon as I get him and his family safe I'll call you back. I mean what I say, Cade. I have a good relationship with your master and I won't have that hurt because I'm doing something behind his back."

"I understand, Mr. Wolff. As soon as I can I'll let all of them know. I don't have...I don't have a lot of money, but I'll pay you for this. I need to make sure that Paul and his family are safe."

He assured her they would be and they hung up after he told her that she would only owe him an explanation. Paul called her back almost two minutes later. While she was on the phone with him Bradley showed up. When she hung up Cade sat there for several minutes wondering how her life had gotten so bad. Picking up the phone again she called Gabe. He wasn't happy.

"I'm sending you the file we want moved. As soon as it's moved and I have confirmation that it's done you'd better watch your back. I'm going to enjoy killing you. I'm going to kill you slowly and with relish."

"You know, you shouldn't threaten someone you need something from, you moronic jackass. I'm moving this, but you know this, I—"

"No, you know this. I'm not threatening you. I'm making you a promise. You are a dead woman."

Cade asked Duncan if he'd take her to the Post Office. She could have taken a car she was sure, but to be honest, she wasn't sure she could drive. She was shaking so hard that she knew that she'd have an accident if she tried.

"Miss, if you don't mind my saying, you look as though you are in trouble. The master is a good man. He would help you with whatever is happening. He and her ladyship are very good people."

Cade knew that he was right. What scared her the most was what Shawn would say when he found out what she was. A thief. And she was sure that no matter what Gabriel had done to make her do it she was still the one who had done it. The one who had been moving millions and millions of dollars for this man for years. Sighing heavily, she went in to pick up the package. When she got back to the mansion she went into the dining room and opened it up.

"Mother fuck. I'm so screwed."

At sunset Cade was still sitting in the dining room. She'd only gotten up once and that was to go to the bathroom. She knew that Duncan had come in several times and checked on her, but she didn't answer him. She knew that he was worried, but she couldn't help him. When he came in again she asked him to please let the master know that she needed to speak to him in private.

"Miss? His lordship said that Master Shawn will need to be present as well. I have sent for him. My master said for me to take you to the study while we wait. Is there anything that I may get for you? You have not taken any foods or liquids today and you are now the mate to a vampire and will need to keep your health up."

Cade wondered how long that would last. Once they found out what she was and what she had to do they would probably feed her to the wolves. A small laugh escaped and she hurried to cover it up. It probably wouldn't do if she lost it now. Aaron was sitting behind his desk when she entered.

"I just spoke to Bradley. He is on his way here too. It seems you've been a very busy girl today. He said to tell you that the Chrismans are safe and that it's time for you to pay up. I don't like being in the dark when it comes to asking for help. Next time you need someone helped, you ask me first. If I can't help you, then you go to someone else. This is not a good way to start a relationship with me, Cade. I don't like surprises."

"Then this is really going to piss you off. If it means anything at all, I'm sorry. Not about calling Mr. Wolff, but for bringing this to your house. I never meant...maybe we should wait on the others. They aren't going to be any happier than you are."

Shawn arrived first. He crossed the room and pulled her into his arms. She let him. If this was going to be the last time he held her then she wanted it to last. When he tried to get her to tell him what was going on she simply shook her head. He held her until the alpha arrived. Aaron asked Shawn to close and lock the door.

"I'm going to start from the beginning if that's okay. You can ask me whatever you want and I'll answer as best I can. I want you all to know that I'm sorry. So very sorry about all of this." She took a deep breath and started her tale. "When I was ten I figured out I could use the computer in ways that it was never made for. Well, I didn't discover it, Garrett did. I had no idea that everyone couldn't do the same thing. Anyway, I could bounce. I know that doesn't make any sense to you, but I don't know what else to call what I can do. I...yes?" Mr. MacManus raised his hand.

"If this is computer related I feel we should bring in our own expert. I for one want to make sure that we are all on the same page. Pete can be here in an instant if you don't have her far away." Aaron looked at Bradley.

"No, she's at the pack house. Just call her. I'm sure whatever she's doing she'll be glad to come and help out."

In less than three minutes Pete Marshall was sitting at the desk that Aaron had given up for her and the computer was humming. She smiled at Cade. Cade just looked away. One more person to know of her humiliation. She wondered if Sara or any of the others should be invited in and clamped down on that thought. She was the one who had screwed up, not these people. She had no rights at the moment.

Cade looked back at Pete. The woman had the most beautiful artwork on her face and neck. A very vivid vine of ivy went across her left eye and down around her neck. Both her arms were also covered in the vine. Cade wondered how far it went down her back and if it was everywhere when she noticed that Pete was smiling at her.

"It's everywhere. It's also my sigil, my mark. My mate Dominic has the same thing all over him. When he bit me, he took my powers when I took his. It's my protector. Sometime I'll show you what cool things it can do."

"That's all very fascinating. Cade said she bounces. Would you please tell us what that means so that we can better understand what's going on?" Cade wasn't surprised at the clipped tone in Aaron's voice, but Pete was.

"Well, maybe if I knew more. And drop the tone, blood sucker. I've only been here five minutes and you're already getting on my last nerve. Cade, honey, tell me what you said. The vamps in the room are usually so ready to bite first and ask questions...come to think of it, do you ever clarify when you yell at people, old man?"

Cade looked between the two of them. Neither of them said a word. She had a feeling that these two went on like this a lot. Cade sat down in the chair and started to explain. "I can't be traced. When I sit down at the computer it's like this huge map opens up and I move all over. When this man, the one I'm going to tell you about, first found out he ran some tests. His experts couldn't find me. I was either much too fast for them to track or never stayed in the same place long enough to get a good fix on my location."

"Really? That's so cool. Here, come and show me. I have my laptop with me. Hang on a sec while I...hey, fuzz ball, do you think you can get us something to drink? I sure could use a big glass of tea."

"We don't have time for social hour, Pete. Just have her show you what's going on and let's get his over with. I'm not a happy man right now," Aaron said.

Pete winked at Cade and looked at Aaron. "When the hell are you a happy camper? I was trying to be nice, but I guess you can't get that through your thick skull. Go away. Give us about ten and then come back."

Cade watched as the two of them stared at one another. She was sure this wasn't going to end well and for the life of her she didn't know who the winner would be. After a few more tense seconds Aaron stood and left the room. Bradley, laughing and trying his best not to show it, followed.

Shawn sat still. "I'm not leaving. I don't know what's going on, but I'm not leaving. You can have your little girl talk if you need to and I won't say a word."

Cade looked at Pete. When she shrugged Cade relaxed. She wanted Shawn to stay, but there was no way she was going to ask. The woman frankly terrified her. Ten minutes later the door opened again and Aaron, Bradley, and Duncan walked in. Duncan had a large tray in his hands and once he'd set it down he left immediately. Pete leaned back in the office chair with a large plate of foodstuff and the largest glass of iced tea Cade had ever seen.

"Cade's right, she bounces. Not only that, but she can break down any security system I know, even mine. In less than two minutes she not only broke into our accounts, but no matter what I threw in her way as a blocker, she circumvented it and moved in. It's as if her mind is connected to the computer and it works with her. If what she can do fell into the wrong hands, then heaven help them. She is a walking nightmare for anyone with any kind of computer access."

"Is this what this is about, Cade? That man, the one who threatened your friends, he knows what you can do and he threatened them to make you do something? How long? How long has this been happening?" She wanted to crawl up into Shawn's lap and answer him, but knew that he'd be pissed when she answered.

She lowered her head. "Ever since Garrett caught me trying to change my grades in high school."

CHAPTER 13

"I was changing my grades a long time before he caught me, but when he did he decided that I should change his as well. Only he wanted the higher marks. I knew it wasn't right, but he wasn't going to graduate if I didn't do something. I had hoped that he'd leave home once he got out of school, but time after time he'd come back until our par...his parents were killed."

"You were lowering your grades? Why? Why would you lower your grades and make his higher?" Shawn asked her softly.

"I was thirteen and they wanted to put me in the pre-college classes. The other kids made fun of me. Garrett's parents made me...they were ashamed of me. So I changed them. It wasn't hard."

Shawn walked over and picked her up. She was snuggled in his lap and held tight. She wanted to cry, wanted to sob that it wasn't fair, but she just let him hold her. When Aaron cleared his throat she turned and continued. "Garrett was...special. At least that's what his parents said to me. Every time he'd hit me, hurt me in some way, or if I didn't give in to him, they'd make me do what he wanted. Mom, his mom, told me that I needed to never hurt him, that he was never going to be much and anything I could do to help him would be for the best. I...I was beaten when he didn't get his way, even if I didn't have anything...I'm sorry. This has nothing to do with what happened today.

"Then one day Garrett came to me and told me that I needed to get him some money. That he owed someone a lot of it and if they didn't get their money he was going to be killed. I didn't want to do it, but his father made me. He'd beaten me until I couldn't move. The next day I moved almost twenty thousand dollars from someone's account at the bank to Garrett's account. He didn't even say thanks. Then two weeks later he was back again. I tried to fight him about it, but he'd hurt me so badly that I just did it instead of having him beat me up.

"Then I was arrested. I hadn't done anything wrong, at least not where anyone could catch me. But this cop, Gabriel Sheets, told me that I was going to start working for him and his friends. Garrett had told him what I could do in exchange for some of his gambling debts. I refused. He told me that if I didn't help, something would happen to my friend and her granddaughter. Gabriel said that if I didn't help, he'd kill them."

"He did, didn't he? He killed them because you wouldn't help them. And then he told you about it."

Cade had forgotten anyone other than Aaron was in the room with her so when Bradley spoke she jumped. She knew that Shawn was there, but she had been telling this to Aaron and had simply been focusing on him.

"Yes. He and Garrett. The next day after he let me go Gabriel came by my house and told me that someone had told Ida before she was killed that I'd been the one who caused their deaths and that I was responsible. I had no choice after that. If I balked then he'd threaten someone else.

"Paul let me go at the diner and then Gabriel couldn't get in touch with me. When he couldn't, he kidnapped Paul's daughter so that I would do this job for him. That's why I called Bradley. I couldn't...I didn't want him to hurt them. I'm sorry. I told him that this would be the last job."

"You don't really think he's going to quit, do you? You can't think that he's going to be okay with his cash hog just telling him she's had enough? Christ, Cade, he's either going to keep going and kill more and more people you know, or he has to be stopped. I'm all for stopping his ass."

Cade smiled at Bradley. He was so fierce now. Before he wanted to beat her she was sure, but now he was her ally.

"No. I don't think he's going to quit. And now he's involved you, Mr. MacManus.

~~~

Shawn looked over the paper work that Cade had picked up at the Post Office today. He was trying to work past the anger and focus on the issue at hand, but it was hard. He realized that about the time she had been telling him what she wanted to do to him, distracting him, she was planning to go out without him and to probably take on this man on her own.

When Cade had gotten up to go to the bathroom again, he'd gotten up too. When she returned he made sure he was standing when she entered. He would never forget the look that passed over her face when he didn't go to her, but she moved to the desk when Pete had asked her to come and show her something. He'd caught Aaron looking at him oddly a couple of times, but he chose to ignore it. At least for now.

Shawn looked at the information again. Cade was to move all of the money in this account into another. All the money in Aaron's account was to be moved to an account in an off shore account for Gabriel. According to the information, Cade was to move the money by noon tomorrow or face the consequences.

Pete and Cade had been working on a plan to make it look like Cade moved the money. Shawn had no idea if they could make it work. He didn't know why they didn't have Cade just tell Gabriel that she moved it and then watch him until he made a mistake. Seemed to Shawn that Gabriel was pretty stupid so it wouldn't be a long wait to get him to make one. He was deep in thought when Aaron sat down next to him.

"You all right? You look at her any harder and she'll turn to stone. Want to talk about it? I'm a pretty good listener."

Shawn looked over at Aaron. "She lied to me. She told me that everything was all right this morning when I felt her anger. How can I trust her when she keeps something like this from me? How the hell am I suppose to keep her safe if she won't tell me what's going on?"

"So you've told her everything? You've told her that you've gotten all of your memory back?" Shawn looked sharply at Aaron as he continued. "Yeah, I'm aware of that. I can tell by the way you're talking, the way that you're moving, that you've remembered. I told you, I'm a good listener."

Shawn glanced at Aaron then at Cade again. She wouldn't look at him anymore. Not that he could blame her. Every time he'd caught her looking at him he glared at her. He wasn't even sure if he had any right to be mad and that made him madder.

"I got it back right after I bit her. We are a couple now, both mated and bonded. And as soon as we mated it was as if my mind opened up and all this information flooded it. I know why I was coming here. I'll talk to you about it later, but this...how can I be there for her? How can I help her when she's not going to do what I want her to do? I'm in love with her and I can't keep her safe."

"And you won't be able to. Not from everything. You think she was just sitting around waiting for you to come along and start bossing her around? Yeah, we boss. I get told that a lot by Sara. I know this is a cliché, but pick your battles. She left here when you told her to stay. What happened? I found out that I'm her next target. You know about Gabriel Sheets. We know how brilliant she is and we've gained her trust."

"Trust? How do you figure that?" Shawn looked back over at the women when Pete burst out laughing. He wasn't sure what they were talking about, but Cade was blushing. It must have been good.

"You don't think it was easy for her to come and tell her new master that she is supposed to steal all my money, do you? Even mated to you I'm still more powerful than her. She came to me before you were up and she had to know that I could have ripped her throat out before you'd have gotten here to save her. She sat on your lap even though she knew that she had lied to you. Again, she must know that you're stronger and even you could have hurt her."

"I can't hurt her. I won't hurt her either. Okay, so she trusted me not to rip her throat out. Maybe she knows that I can't harm her."

As soon as he said it he realized it wasn't true. He knew that what she'd done was seek comfort from him and he'd given it. At least until he'd gotten pissed and had practically thrown her off his lap. "Christ, you always this annoying? Tell me again why we're friends? I can't have been happy hanging around with someone who thinks they're right all the time."

"I don't think I'm right, I am right. You might want to remember that too. Of course, if you tell Sara she'll just tell you that I'm wrong. Damned woman disagrees with me just to be pertinacious."

Shawn just laughed. He looked back over to Cade and caught her looking at him. His body tightened with need. Without taking his eyes off her he spoke to Aaron. "I need her. I want to...do you think you can figure out a way to end this meeting now? So I can... I have to take her to our lair and grovel."

Aaron jumped up so quickly that Shawn jumped too. "All right, meeting over. Shawn, go fuck Cade so we can move on. I'm going to find my mate and do the same. I would suggest that you two do the same." Aaron pointed to Pete and Bradley. "We have a lot of work to do and we do much better if we're relaxed."

Everyone cleared out in seconds. Everyone but Cade and Shawn. She was still sitting at the desk and he was still standing at the sofa.

He looked at the door as it closed, then back at Cade. "I'm going to kill him tomorrow. I thought about staking him in the sun, but I think he'd just order the sun to not rise until he could convince us all to come to our senses and release him. Then he'd find some way of making it all our fault that he's a pain in the ass."

Cade laughed, which was what he had hoped she'd do. He moved slowly toward her and unbuttoned his shirt as he went. The lair seemed too far away, much too far away, and he didn't want to wait.

"I'm a fool. And before you agree let me explain. I should have asked you to stay here, not demanded. And I should have been there for you, not pushed you away. You've had a hell of a couple of weeks and I haven't made it any better. I'm sorry." Shawn's shirt came off and he unsnapped his pants as he toed off his shoes. He'd not put on any socks nor any briefs because Aaron had made it seem imperative that he get to the study right when he said.

Cade licked her lips and his cock jumped. When she opened her mouth and he could see her fangs beginning to drop he nearly whimpered with need. Leaving his pants at his hips, he dropped to his knees in front of her.

"Take off your blouse. Please? I want to see you, feel you."

Her fingers shook as she worked the buttons through the holes. When it was open she pulled it off her shoulders and cupped her bare breasts. His cock ached. When he moved closer to her she opened her legs to let him in. Cupping his hands over hers he lifted both her hands and her breasts up. Lowering his head he took the hard nipple in his mouth and nipped at it gently. Her moan was rough and long.

"Please, Shawn. I need you. I want you."

When she wove her fingers into his hair and pulled him tighter to her he opened his mouth wider over her breast and sucked hard. She arched into him and tightened her grip in his hair. Shawn moved his hands down her ribs then over her hips to her ass. Pulling her forward, she wrapped her legs around his ribs and held him.

"Stand up, baby. I want to take your pants off and taste you. The smell of your arousal is making me wild with the need to taste you."

"No. Not this time. It's my turn. You stand up and take your pants off. I want to taste your cum. I want to feel your cock in my mouth."

She dropped her legs from around him and pushed him back. He wasn't sure if she had lifted him up or he just moved without realizing it. But suddenly he was up and leaning against the desk and she was running her fingers up his ribs and over his nipples. When she tweaked one of them he growled deep in his chest.

"Don't play too long little girl. I'm a man with a powerful need to mate with you. If you keep this up you could find yourself leaning over that chair with my cock deep inside of you. Take me, Cade. Take me in your mouth and suck me."

Shawn watched as she gripped the zipper to his pants in her teeth and pulled it down. His cock moved over her cheeks as she rubbed against him. The drop of pre-cum at the tip was quickly lapped up when she ran her tongue around the blood engorged head.

"Baby, please. You're killing me. I'm not going to be responsible for what happens if you don't take me now."

His head felt as if it blew off his shoulders a moment later when she wrapped her lips around him. His fangs dropped with the need to taste her; his eyes darkened so deep he couldn't make out any other colors but the red haze. Grabbing the back of her head he held her to him as he moved in the heat of her mouth.

Cade's tongue was relentless. She swirled it around and around him until he was sure she had several tongues moving over him and not just the one. When she licked him along the heavy, pulsing vein and down his length he felt his balls tighten, his spine tingle with the need to come. Guiding her head back up to his cock she took him deep. He didn't want to hurt her, but he couldn't seem to stop fucking her mouth hard. When Cade reached between his legs and rolled his tight sac in her palm he came. Harder and faster he pumped, filling her mouth, her throat with his seed. When the last wave shot from his cock he jerked her head away and pulled it up to his. Devouring her mouth, he moved them to the floor. Need made him not care what happened to her clothing. Her jeans ripped from her body even as she wrapped herself around him.

"No. Over. Over onto your belly. I'm going to fuck you, Cade. And when you come, I'm going to bite. I'm going to bite hard and drink from you."

Cade moved to the floor quicker. She may have said something, he wasn't sure, but the roaring in his head, the blood pounding through his body, made him an animal. His beast rose up and he couldn't stop it if he tried.

When her ass was raised up before him he grabbed her hips and slammed deep. Her pussy, hot and soaked, took him. Her answering primal cry gave him added strength. He slammed again and again, gripping her hips so tightly he knew in the back of his mind she'd wear a bruise because of him. She didn't pull away. With every surge forward she rammed back just as hard, taking him deeper into her heat. Leaning forward, nipping hard at her shoulder, he growled in her ear.

"Come. Come now." And she did. When she screamed out his name Shawn pulled her body up to his and took her throat. His bite was deep, deeper than he'd ever bit anyone during sex before. Her blood exploded in his mouth. Hot, spicy, and thick, it filled his body. When she came again he reached around and gave her his wrist. Her bite then her first draw sent him over the edge again.

As her body continued to come down Shawn licked the wound at her throat closed and held her. When she sealed the wounds at his wrist he simply held her to him, listening to her heart as it slowed and her breathing returned to normal. He loved her. Loved her with all his soul and didn't know what he'd do if anything ever happened to her.

Kissing her neck, only then realizing she was asleep, he lifted her body from his and, pulling shadows around them, transported them to their lair. Gently laying her into the bed he smiled at how beautiful she looked lying there. Kissing her again he left her to sleep and rest while he went in search of Aaron.

Chapter 14

Gabriel hit the man again. Damn it, why couldn't he just fucking do as he'd been told? One simple thing, find his sister and bring her to him. Garrett's head rolled to the side as blood poured from the cuts on his face. Gabriel wanted to hit him again, but didn't want to kill him. At least not yet. Once Cade was in his hands Garrett could cease to exist for all Gabriel cared. He heard the scraping sound of someone coming to the door just before the knock. Bidding Toby Mare entrance, Gabriel moved to the sink to wash Garrett's blood from his hand.

"Did you find that restaurant owner? Or his kid? Hell, right now I'd be happy with the kid who delivers their papers."

Chrisman and his family had disappeared practically as soon as he'd had the daughter returned to them. When he'd sent his crew back to the house to kill them they had been gone. There were too many scents to make a positive ID on who had taken them, but wolf was prevalent all over the grounds. He swore to himself if Cade had a wolf pack protecting the Chrismans not only would she pay, but they would as well.

"Nothing, sir. The restaurant is closed up tight with an 'illness in family' sign in the window and nothing around town either. One lady seemed to think someone had been ill for a long time. Anyway, I got a feeler out like you said on the pack. I'm not so sure you wanna fuck with them. Heard tell that their alpha is one mean-assed mother fucker. Also, did you know that we are in their territory? Ain't we supposed to, I don't know, let 'em know we be hunting on their—"

Gabriel hit him. Hit him hard enough that he ended up across the room. Gabriel noticed that he was lying at an odd angle and that his neck looked bent. For some reason that pissed Gabriel off too. He had no time to try and find another second right now and this fucker Toby had to know that before he'd made Gabriel kill him. He walked over and kicked Toby's dead body again.

Gabriel hated being told no, but he hated being told he was in the wrong even more. He was alpha and, as such, this pack leader would bow before him. And if this so called 'bad mother fucker' wasn't careful Gabriel would have this territory all his own too.

Picking up the bucket of water he had sitting next to the chair where Garrett was tied Gabriel tossed the contents over Garrett. He sputtered and moaned, but eventually came awake. His left eye was cut badly and swollen shut. His right wasn't much better, but he would be able to see out of it. For a little while at least. Blood stained his shirt and the lap of his jeans. Gabriel looked, was pleased to see he had an erection, and nearly dropped down and took him into his mouth, but he had things to do first. Later, he promised himself. Later, he'd go down on Garrett and make him suffer some more.

"I need you to find her. This is your last chance. Fuck this up and it will be the last thing you ever do. If you don't bring her back to me in five days I'll hunt you down and rip your throat out. You understand me?"

Garrett's jaw was probably hurting like hell, but Gabriel didn't care. He waited for an answer that was almost too low to hear. Gabriel was enjoying this more than he had anything in a long, long time.

"Yeths. I untherstath. Peths don't hith me again. Peths? I'll thine her. I promiths. I'll thine her."

Gabriel looked at the man in disgust as he staggered toward the door. Garrett had become a liability and his usefulness in controlling his sister was no longer helping. Gabriel hoped that Garrett would fail just so that he could have the pleasure of killing him. Then he smiled. Since when did he need an excuse to kill someone simply for the pleasure of it? Moving to his desk Gabriel called in a couple of rogues that he knew would help him make the alpha understand that a new king was in town.

~~~

"I'm not sure. I guess you'd have to take into consideration that he's been reining for centuries and no one has ever had the nerve to challenge him before. I'm not saying I want to or even that I could, but enough is enough."

Shawn and Aaron had been talking about Ferris Tilton for two hours and they were no closer to knowing what had to be done than before. It was obvious that something had to be done, but what was the question. Aaron seemed to think that Shawn could do it, while he didn't.

"What is it that makes you think you couldn't win against him? You're older and by far more powerful. Smarter in ways that he could never obtain. You have a great sense of integrity and you have a moral compass that would never let you do the things he's been doing. If nothing else, Shawn, you have to do it for those humans."

Shawn had discovered that Ferris was snatching women off the streets and turning them—or trying to turn them anyway. The ones that lived would be put with several males until she got pregnant. Shawn and Aaron both knew that the likelihood of that happening was slim to none. The chances of one of the males being a mate to the female being just one factor and the other, without the bond between them, a child could never be conceived. After three or four months of unsuccessful attempts Ferris would give the girl to one of his butt buddies to use as he saw fit. Most of the time they were used as a source of food or a sexual plaything that more often than not ended in her death, whether by suicide or starvation. Either way, they didn't last long.

"It's not that I don't think I couldn't win. I'm not thinking that, but how do I clean house? The Council won't allow me to murder my own kind and I'm not stupid enough to think that once I am master my life would not be in constant danger. Now with Cade, that has just doubled my chances of having one of them try to take me out."

The Council of Vampires was newly formed, at least to these two vampires. It had been around for only about three hundred years. There had always been a court of sorts before, but it was usually run by a group of men who had nothing better to do than to sit judgment on some issue brought to them. And the side with the most money or influence came out the winner every time. Now it was a set group of vampire that were paid by the queen, Mel. She had final say on all proceedings and her judgment was swift and sound. There had been less and less need for the Council to be brought together since she had enacted the set of rules governing them all.

"I would still take it before Mel. She is fair and will listen to you. It has to stop. We don't want to cause an all out war between us and the humans. You and I both know what will happen if that becomes fact. While we aren't exactly mainstream now we can at least move within the circles of humans and not be staked at every turn. If this gets out that we are killing humans, especially human women, for the kill then we will have major problems again."

Shawn knew that Aaron was right. Shawn even knew that before he came here Aaron would tell him just what he had. The problem was, he still didn't know what to do. He would go before Mel and let her know, but as for whether he'd challenge Ferris, that was something he couldn't do right now.

~~~

Cade sat at the computer and waited for Pete to give her the signal. She was really going to do it. She was going to take all the money out of Mr. MacManus' bank accounts and put it into Gabriel's. Well, not really. The bank had worked with Pete to set up a dummy account to remove the "money" from.

"See, the numbers are almost the same except for these two numbers are reversed. Most people wouldn't even notice the numbers are different because the first and last are what they should be. I'm hoping this guy won't notice either. When he receives the confirmation that you moved the money he'll use the same link to move this money out. Only it's not going anywhere."

"How is that going to help? I mean, won't he notice that there isn't any money in the account when he goes to take it out?" Cade knew that she would notice that there was suddenly no money. She didn't have any to begin with so that would be an indicator to her. She had no idea how much money was in the accounts, but she was reasonably sure it was more than she had.

"By the time he figures it out I'll have him. I'm going to track the money that's moved out of the bogus account and then see where it leads. We'll be able to see what he's doing with the money and who else might be playing with him. See?"

Cade didn't, but she didn't really think anyone would. Pete was really sweet and Cade liked her, but she wasn't sure of most of what she was saying. When she looked at Aaron for guidance he just winked at her. Not a lot of help. So when Pete told her to "jack it to the max" she turned back to the computer and hoped that she was supposed to move the money.

Touching the mouse gave her peace. Cade had never figured out why it did, but she felt like she could do anything when she held a piece of technology in her hand. She may not have understood the ins and outs of it, but it felt right. Moving the mouse to the link in the bank she began the process of getting into the locked account. Energy flowed down her arm and through her fingers.

When Cade bounced, as she'd told Pete, she literally did bounce. Her IP or Internet Protocol address never stayed stationary. It would alight on one address and stay for an indeterminate amount of time before moving to the next. So that if one was trying to pinpoint where she was working from a person would have to follow her to the next place she hit. Then by the time that person got there she may have moved on to ten or more addresses by then. Since her mind was working the addresses and not her computer there was never a set pattern. She vaguely heard Pete tell someone behind her that Cade had been to Paris and to Switzerland and she'd already changed her IP eighty-four times in the thirty-eight minutes she'd been working.

"If I wasn't trying to keep up with her," Pete said, "I'd never believe it was possible. She is a computer hacker's best friend and a security system's worst enemy. Its small wonder that this guy hasn't tried to kidnap her and make her sit at a computer all day just moving money out of any account he wants. Christ, when you think of what she could do if she were in the wrong hands it's just fucking scary."

Cade turned back to them when she was finished. Now all they had to do was wait on the bank or Gabriel to let them know what happened next. Cade looked over at Shawn and spoke to the room in general, but never took her eyes off him. She needed to know his reaction.

"He did. Kidnap me once. I was coming home from work when he had one of his cronies pick me up in his cruiser and take me to Gabe. I was terrified and sick when he locked me in this room. There were no windows, nothing but a desk, computer, and a cot. I couldn't...no matter what he did to me, I couldn't work. The second time the computer exploded when I touched it he tried putting me in another place. This one had windows, a scene out the one that was beautiful. But my mind refused to work for him. It...I shut down."

"What did he do to you, baby? He didn't just lock you in a room, did he? Tell me what else he did to you."

Shawn's voice was low and hard. She wasn't afraid for herself, she knew that he wasn't mad at her. But fear, fear for what might happen to him if he tangled with Gabe. When she didn't answer right away he got up, kneeled before her, and took her hand into his.

"He said...he said that he'd kill them, my par...Garrett's parents. I knew that they didn't much care for me, but they were all I had. So I tried to cooperate, I really did. But I couldn't make it work. I couldn't even touch the computer without it frizzing out. He was so angry, so very...he's a wolf. I didn't know that before, but he was so mad at me that he changed. I couldn't...I couldn't work after that. He was so huge and he tried to bite me." She was startled when Shawn brushed away the tears. She hadn't realized she was even crying until then. His quick kiss made her feel good.

"Baby, I don't want to frighten you either, but when I find him, and I will, I'm going to rip his fucking throat out and feast on his blood. Then I'm going to tear him apart."

Shawn's voice was so calm, so soft. He could have been telling her that he loved her or that he was going to pick up milk on the way home tonight. She didn't know why, but she found this to be more terrifying than anything she'd witnessed so far.

"Are you saying that this Gabriel person is a werewolf? And he's here? Holy shit! I wonder if Bradley knows. It's against council rules to come into another supe's territory without asking for permission. I think I'll give my friend a good heads up."

Aaron's warning came a little too late. The rogues that Gabriel had sent to the pack house had already been there. And Bradley was not a happy alpha.

CHAPTER 15

"They actually came on my land and threatened me. Me! Of all the nerve. I have the largest pack in the United States and they threatened me," Bradley said yet again. His mate, Airic, had heard it more than them and she was showing her need for him to move on.

"Yes, dear. We know. You've been telling us all for the past hour. Eat your apple dumpling before I do. It's been sitting there in front of you long enough. And I'm still hungry."

The play between the alpha and his bitch was bordering on hysterical. Aaron had invited them for dinner when Bradley had told him that he'd had a visitor.

Four rogues had showed up just as breakfast was starting and had broken into the pack house during the monthly breakfast meeting. They'd barely gotten through the broken down front door when three of them were killed and the fourth was only still alive because Charlie Wolff, Bradley's grandfather, had stopped them with a loud howl.

"Maybe we outta ask them why they're here before we go killing them all, don't you think? Could help us, gee, I don't know, know if there are anymore out there just waiting to come in the broken door. Stupid pups. Back in my day we'd have captured them all four and then had fun torturing them."

"I know, Grandda. I'll have a talk with them. We should have better manners when someone comes into my home and tries to kill me. Next time I'll have Martha bake up some pies for them to eat along with my throat."

"No point in getting snarly with me, young man. You still ain't too old for me to take out to the woodshed. I'm just saying that we could get more from a living wolf than a dead one."

When Aaron had heard this story between Bradley and his grandda he'd laughed for a good twenty minutes.

"You know, you'd do well to beef up your own security, fang face. And Grandda did have a point. We can't get information from a dead guy. If you're killed then I'm not going to know who to thank."

Aaron was glad for Bradley's friendship. Otherwise, he may have had to drain him. The two of them had been snipping at one another since the beginning. Aaron hoped they would continue to do so.

"If the two of you are finished we need to talk about this money situation." Pete sat down as she spoke and tried to take the last dumpling from Airic, which got her growled at. "The bank said that the money is still sitting there. Cade, does it normally move right away or does he move it later? Anything you can tell us would be great."

Pete was perhaps the greatest computer person Aaron knew. She'd been working for Bradley as their online computer security expert since she'd mated with Dominic. She was also a powerful wood nymph.

"I don't know anything about the money once I move it. I try to get my money up front, but lately it's been difficult. I'd quit the other day when Gabriel hadn't paid me in a while. I got a portion of what he owed me in the form of a check. That's when he threatened Paul's family the first time. Then when he couldn't contact me this time he kidnapped Paul's daughter."

"Wait. He paid you with a check? Please tell me you still have it. If we can get the account number off of it then we are that much closer to getting him," Pete said.

"I don't know what I did with it. I could look for you. Maybe it's in the apartment over the diner. I could go and get it for you if you'd like."

Before Aaron could tell her no Shawn jumped up. Aaron almost felt sorry for Shawn. He was going to do something very stupid like demand that Cade stay here and he'd go get it. Aaron knew from experience that the women of this generation responded much better to asking than they did demanding.

"You still demand, you arrogant ass. Why just yesterday you demanded that I not leave the estate. I don't need you to do everything for me, you know."

Aaron smiled when Sara whispered through his mind. "Yes, you do. But I certainly made it worth your while to wait for me, didn't I? I believe you came seven times before I had my own release. I tried for eight, but you were simply too tired, you said."

"Aaron, I came eleven times and that isn't the point. A person needs to recuperate when they have that many clim...you are changing the subject. I want you to stop demanding that I do as you say when you say it."

"Yes dear. I will give it my best." They both knew that he wouldn't, as much as they knew that Shawn would be in trouble as soon as the words for Cade to stay in the house slipped from his mouth. Cade shimmered with anger in an instant.

"You won't tell me what to do, you overgrown ass. I have a mind and I'm very good at using it. I will go where I want, when I want, and for as long as I want." Cade poked Shawn in the chest with each word.

Aaron didn't want to laugh, he really didn't, but it was just great to see one of his best friends being brow beaten by his mate. When she had Shawn backed against the wall he growled. Cade didn't miss a beat and growled right back at him. Her fangs dropped and her eyes turned. When he laughed again, Cade turned on him.

"You think this is funny? Why are you all so friggin' bossy all the time? Is it because you're, like, as old as dirt? I want you all to know this right now. I don't need any of you to watch over me like I'm some sort of baby. I was doing just fine, not great, but just fine."

"Cade, I don't think what you're feeling is funny. It's that I've known Shawn for so long and to see a slip of a woman brow beating him into a corner makes me laugh. I must admit that I, too, have a bit of a problem with my arrogance, or so I've been told." He paused at Sara's snort. He would deal with her later. "But Shawn and I have been around since women were at home with the children. Where men protected their mates, their families, with all that they were, even giving up their lives for them if necessary. I'm sure if you give Shawn enough time he'll be just as relaxed and as easy as I am."

Another snort, this one from Pete, made him frown at them. Damn it, he was a changed man. Just when he was about to continue his explanation of just how he'd changed Pete's cell phone rang.

"That was the bank. The money is on the move."

~~~

Cade was sitting in the kitchen when the children came in. She was so happy to have their laughter that she made them breakfast of whatever they wanted. Duncan just fussed and told her that she was not supposed to cook now, that Miss Penny would be in shortly.

"I need this, Duncan. I need to keep busy or I may run screaming out of the house. I'm sure Miss Penny won't mind at all. And I promise that I'll clean up my mess when I'm done."

"You will do nothing of the sort, Lady Cade. I will make sure the kitchen in is pristine condition when you are finished. I will, however, insist that you must be careful around that washer. Yesterday it took one of her ladyship's new sweaters and made it the size of one of Miss Lizzy's dollies. I believe it to be possessed."

Cade laughed and kissed Duncan on the cheek. She really liked this man. He was sweet and endearing. She wanted to bundle him up in her pocket and pull him out again when she was sad. She hoped that he never changed. And she was sure that he wouldn't.

"Thank you, Lady Cade. You should strive to not kiss too many males in the future. Master Shawn is a very jealous man, as all vampires are. I do believe that he would indeed pull my liver up through my nose and then eat it." Duncan grinned at her when she stared at him speechless. "I heard that said on one of the shows I watch. I cannot imagine the amount of skill it would take to perform such a feat, do you?"

She had to bite her inner cheek hard. "No. No, I can't say that I could. I need to go into town, Duncan. Do you think it would be all right if I got my bike out of the garage? I won't be long. Just long enough to run to the diner and back."

"Oh no, miss. You must not anger Master Shawn. He was quite specific on you staying here today. He will be most displeased with us both if I allow you to leave."

"Duncan, I really like you. But if you go all caveman on me, too, I might have to hurt someone. I'm going into town. You can tell Shawn I made you let me go."

Cade had had enough of the stupid ordering her around. Grabbing up her coat she moved to the door and then to her bike. The closer she got to it, the slower her steps became.

"Damn him all to hell!" Shawn had taken her tires off. And not only that, but there was a nice note on the seat addressed to her.

"Stay here. If I even hear that you left I will beat that cute little bottom of yours until you can't sit for a week. Love, Shawn."

Cade crumpled up the note and stood there. She could go back in the house and ask Duncan to take her to town. She could hotwire a car in the massive garage and drive herself. But she knew that Aaron would have her arrested for grand larceny if she did that. Or she could walk. Walking sounded good. Maybe by the time she got to town and to the diner she'd be cooled off enough to speak to Shawn again. By the time she got to the end of the drive she was pretty sure that walking wasn't going to save the arrogant ass from getting a piece of her mind. And when she was perhaps three miles from town she was positive that he was going to hurt for a few days when she was finished with him.

Cade had a key to the diner so she let herself in. She loved the smell of the place. And when she made her way into the diner area she went to the pop machine, got herself a drink, and sat down just to look around and rest. She didn't know how many miles it was to here, but her feet hurt and she was exhausted. Sitting in one of the nine booths around the room she looked around.

The theme was the fifties. Pictures and posters of rock bands from that era were all over the walls. Elvis Presley and Buddy Holly graced more than a few posters and concert reminders. There was even a life-sized cardboard cutout of the King himself from his thinner days. Behind the counter, high on the wall, was a guitar that Paul had told her was a Fender. Cade wasn't sure what the big deal about it was, but everyone who knew anything about music that came in had marveled about the bright blue wonder.

The jukebox in the corner was an antique. Paul and his wife had gotten it as a wedding gift from one of his friends all those years ago. With tender care and loving hands the thing worked as well today as it had back in the day. Cade knew that Paul had been in a band, The Lemon-Aides, and she'd been told that one or two of their forty-fives were behind the glass and bright lights.

The dining area had nine booths around the outside of it. Black and red leather seats and red and black Formica table tops looked worn and soft. The stools around the bar were alternating red and black too. Each booth had a straw container, glass salt and pepper shakers, and catsup when they were open. Black and white tile floors were bright and shiny even in the dim early afternoon sun. Cade smiled as she drank her pop. She loved this place.

When she was finished drinking she went to the cash register and lifted it up. Under it was an envelope with her cash in it and her check from Gabe. With the check she had just under five grand. Not a lot in the world of vampires, she knew, but it was all she had. Stuffing the envelope in the waistband of her jeans she went to the back door and slipped out. She was just locking the door when she felt someone close. The tingle at the back of her neck signaled that someone with magic, she knew what it was now, was close by.

She was just turning around when Gabriel in wolf form was standing behind her. And beyond him were several more wolves. All of them large and several of them with foam dripping from their muzzles. She clutched the keys in her hand wishing with all her might that she could start the day over and stay in the warm bright kitchen with Duncan until Shawn woke up and brought her into town like he said he would. His shift to human form frightened her; his nude body hard and aroused terrified her more.

"Hello Cade, my dear. I think you've been avoiding me. I told you that you would never be rid of me the last time you tried to run. You belong to me." He burrowed his nose at her neck and nipped. Not to draw blood, but to scare her. "Now, come along nicely and I won't have to have these animals behind me tear you to pieces. I don't care if they hurt you, Cade. It's not your body I need, but your mind. Come along nicely and I'll let that stupid brother of yours live a bit longer. Well, long enough to tell you how he killed your mother and took you at any rate."

"My mother? I don't understand. Garrett killed my mother? You lie, Gabe. You'd do anything to make me do—"

Gabriel hit her hard. She felt the blood spurt from her mouth and lip and run down her neck. Her back slammed against the wall as a car roared into the parking lot in front of her.

"I don't lie. I may be a lot of things, but never a liar. Now get in the fucking car, Cade, before I lose my temper. I've had enough of this and I want my money. Why you came to this fucking Podunk town is beyond me." Gabriel dragged her to the back of a large, dark sedan. She was thrown in the back and hit her head again. "When we get to my lair you will do as you're told. I'm not going to put up with any more shit from you. But for now I need quiet."

The rag covered her face before she could move. Cade could smell the sweet smell seconds before she began to drift. Chloroform. He was drugging her with chloroform. She thought about Shawn just before she was out. He was going to be so pissed when he found her.

CHAPTER 16

"Oh Master, I did tell her to stay. She was quite determined to leave. I had thought to take her into town with the car, but she said that I had become a cave dweller and that she would hurt me if I tried. I did not wish to be hurt and I was aware that Master Shawn took her wheels off of her transportation."

Shawn didn't want to take Cade being gone out on Duncan. When Duncan had banged on his door shortly after one o'clock this afternoon Shawn had been in a deep sleep. It had taken him a few minutes to wake up and focus on what Duncan had been saying.

"Lady Cade, she is missing, sire. I have looked everywhere I can think trying to locate her whereabouts, but I have not had any luck. I fear something may have happened to her. I did not have her cell phone number to reach her. I do hope I was correct in waking you, sire."

"Of course, Duncan. Anything that Cade does, you have my permission to wake me. She does tend to get herself into trouble. Let's go and see if we can find her."

That had been two hours ago, still hours before sunset. Shawn knew the real reason she had left was because of him. He paced the large dining room again. Of course that didn't mean he wasn't going to beat her ass when he found her. Right after he made love to her, that was.

"Did she say where she might be going? Was she really upset when she left?" When Aaron raised his brow at him again Shawn tried to temper his tone.

"No, Master Shawn, she did not. When she did not return to the kitchen immediately I had thought she was trying to put the bike back to its original state with tires. I knew that you had taken the screw things with you to the lair and as I did not see her with them I assumed, quite wrongly it would seem, that she wouldn't be able to leave. She was quite upset when she walked out. I thought she would be working off some of her mist for awhile."

Shawn looked at Aaron. Mist? Aaron shrugged gently and turned to Duncan. The poor man was spraying some sort of cleaning stuff over and over on the counter then wiping it away only to do it again. Shawn was sure he was going to wear a place in the heavily-tiled area.

"Steam," Aaron said to Shawn before continuing. "Duncan, what were the two of you talking about before she went outside. Think about it carefully. You said she was upset, about what, do you remember?"

"Yes. Now I remember. She did say that I was not to become a cave dweller. I believe that's what she said, Master Shawn." Duncan sat at the table, pulled out a small bag, and dumped its contents on the table. Six golden spoons poured out. From another pocket he produced a rag and began wiping the spoons with it. "Lady Cade asked to borrow a car, something to go to...I can't remember, sire. She said that if you asked that I was to tell you she made me let her go, that she was forceful. I do believe her to be much stronger than one thinks. She is—the diner! She said that she needed to go to the diner and would return soon."

Shawn sat down. He reached for her mentally again and hit a wall. He didn't feel anything from her. Not death, just a void. The diner, why would she be going to the diner today? As far as he knew the owner, Paul, was still at the pack house with his family. Cade was getting something then. "The check that Pete asked her for. Cade probably went there to get it. She was pissed because I ordered her to stay here and she left to get it on her own. We have to go and see if she's there."

Shawn went to the door and stopped. It was full daylight. He couldn't leave yet. He turned back to Aaron. Before Shawn could say anything Aaron pulled out his cell and called Bradley.

"One of mine is missing. I think she may be at the diner where the human you rescued the other day was at... Thank you, yes. Could I ask a favor of you? Could you send someone there to see if they can find her? I don't believe so. Though that's a thought. I will ask him when I get off from here... You have my thanks." Aaron closed his phone. "Bradley said that he himself will go. He's wondering if the wolves that attacked had anything to do with you, or do you think that they came with this Gabriel person?"

"I don't know any wolves. Well, not really. There were a few stragglers that would come around to do some dirty work for Ferris, but nothing permanent. I can't think of anyone that would be stupid enough to cross me. I do have my moments and, sometimes, I tend to frighten some people."

Shawn reached again. This time he had a touch, brief, but a touch. When he tried to dig in deeper the void moved into his mind. She was alive and afraid. He could feel her moment of fear as though it were his own.

"I touched her just now. Wherever she is, she's afraid. I sense a pack, mostly wolves I think, though there are others—a panther and a bear for sure. Others, too. None are so big or as hungry as the pack."

"I'll let Bradley know when he calls. I'm also bringing Mel here. If Cade is faerie then Mel might be able to locate her quicker than we can. She said that she is coming."

"I'm here. I have her mother's things as well. There is something else. Cade is a Lesser Faerie, but she is also a Golden Faerie. Her mother, Jasmine, was one so, as her birthright, Cade is one. Dad said that she would have a tattoo on her somewhere to mark her." A huge white and gold box appeared on the floor beside her. "There would be a faerie as her sigil, as golden as her birthright. Her father, Vladimir Michaels, also known as Lord Atwell, is still alive. He has been located and is at the castle. I thought I'd let you know before I sent him here."

"Can you find her? I mean, do you have a way of locating her? When I reach I get nothing." The brief touch made Shawn feel hope, but he was still terrified for her.

"While I can't pinpoint her exactly I can give you an idea. Finding her for you is against our laws. The Fates are not happy when you try to adjust what they have set forth. I can tell you that where she is there is magic, black as the deepest hole."

Shawn began to pace. What he really wanted to do was to rant and rave. He wanted to howl at the moon and scream at the injustice of it all. Hunger boiled in his belly. Not for blood, at least not to feed, but to hurt, to avenge, and to kill.

~~~

Cade woke to a dark room. Not just dark, but pitch black. Reaching out she could feel someone in the room with her and then realized it was Garrett. When she tried to move she realized that she had been tied to a chair.

"Where am I, Garrett? You know that you can't make me work this way. I can't work under these kinds of conditions. You know that as well as Gabe."

"He said he'd make you work even if he had to hurt you to do it. You'd better do it, Cade. He's tired of waiting and so are the people he works for." There was a scratching sound then a flare of light from a candle. "I took my money. You need to get me more than this. I can't live off of this little amount and pay off my debts. What were you thinking? You should have a second job or something."

"I don't suppose it occurred to you to get one on your own, did it? You are quite capable of finding a job too. I'm not going to—"

The slap was brutal. He'd hit her before, several times as a matter of fact, but this was stronger. Stars danced in front of her eyes for a few seconds. She looked up at him. He looked different, fuller, and bigger. Reaching a little deeper she could see that he'd been turned. Garrett was now wolf.

"I'm not getting a job. You owe me. I'm tired of telling you how it's going to be, Cade. Its time you started listening to me and doing what I want." He started pacing in front of her. Cade looked around the darkened room.

There was a desk in the corner with what looked like a desktop on it. She could just make out the monitor and the keyboard. There was a lamp on the desk, though it wasn't on, and what appeared to be a vase with a flower in it. The rest of the room was in shadows, but she knew there were no windows and there was only one door. Cade thought she was in a basement; the floor beneath her bare feet was cold and hard. Something occurred to her.

"You are always saying I owe you. Why? What have you done for me that I should be willing to give you all my money and keep you in cash all the time?"

Garrett stopped so suddenly it startled her and then he grinned. She'd seen this grin before. It didn't make her feel good. It looked more like a sneer and she was suddenly very sure she wouldn't want to hear what he said next.

"I did you a favor. Did you know that your mom was a faerie? I mean your real mom, not mine. I saw her with you one time. You were in the park playing with flowers and she was making them grow. Some of them weren't even supposed to be there 'cause I looked it up. You weren't but a baby all bunched up in a big blanket, but you laughed at them."

"I don't see what that has to do with my owing you. So what, I don't remember my mom. Your mother told me that she abandoned me and they took me in." That had always hurt Cade, though she wouldn't tell Garrett that. He already used enough of what he knew about her against her. And the fact that his mother had never seemed to want her hurt more for some reason. His laughter brought her back to the present.

"You weren't abandoned. I killed her. I wanted you to play with me and so I killed her. You look like her, but you are more alive." He laughed at his own joke while Cade tried to wrap her mind around what he'd just said.

"You killed my mother? Why? What did she do to you?"

Garrett sat on the floor in front of her and Cade looked at him, really looked at him. He was insane. His eyes, his mouth, everything about him screamed unbalanced. And he confirmed it with his next statement.

"Mom wouldn't have any more kids. She said it was too dangerous for her. Stupid reason, don't you think? Not to have kids. I wanted someone to play with and she wouldn't give me that. The kids in the neighborhood wouldn't play with me either. They thought I was too mean." Garrett got up to pace again. "I wasn't mean. They were mean. They should have just given me what I wanted. Everybody should just give me what I want and nobody gets hurt."

Cade waited for him to finish. He had always gotten what he wanted even as a young adult. Thinking back on it, Cade thought his parents were afraid of him. She knew she had always been.

"I watched you guys for days and days. You'd be asleep some days and laughing the others. Sometimes there would be some man with her. He would only come really early in the morning, though, and sometimes if you were out late, he'd come to you guys then. Probably your daddy. Then one day when she was all alone I knocked her down. She wasn't very big, not like you."

"You think I owe you because you killed my mother?" Cade stared at him waiting for him to answer her. "You're sick. You fucking bastard, she was my mother. And you killed her because you wanted a playmate. Let me go! Let me go right now."

Garrett put his hands over his ears and started to sing. She screamed louder and he continued to ignore her. A few minutes passed before he sat up on his knees and hit her, this time knocking her back onto the floor behind her. Dizzy, she looked up at him as he stood over her. Magic pooled around them both.

"I wasn't strong before, not like now." He flexed his arm at her before continuing. "I had to hit her and hit her until she let you go. She wouldn't let you go. My hand was hurting and I had to find me something. Finally I found a big stick and I hit her in the head. That made her let go. But I couldn't stop. I liked the sound of the stick hitting her head, the way the blood flew all over the place and landed on me."

Cade started crying now. Her mother had been trying to save her from this sick bastard and he just kept hitting her.

"I took you to my mom. She didn't want you at first. You were all covered in blood and stuff. But I made her. I told her that I could hurt her too. And it was her fault anyway. If she'd just had me another baby I wouldn't have had to hurt her."

"What happened to her...my mom? What happened to her...did you just leave her there?"

"How should I know? I got what I wanted. Or I thought I had. You aren't any better than the kids in school. You didn't want to play with me either. But now you are going to pay me back. You're gonna make me all the money I want when I want it, and Gabriel too. Gabriel is my boss now." Garrett looked confused for a second then smiled at Cade again. "I guess I have a job after all."

Garrett's laughter was crazed and loud. Cade felt the hair on the back of her neck rise and her body curl within itself. Garrett as a wolf was scarier than anything she'd ever known. When he reached down and pulled her back up into a sitting position by grabbing a handful of her hair, she screamed out in pain. She must have startled him because he dropped her and she hit the floor with her head. Pain exploded in her skull, blood splattered on the floor, and everything went black.

CHAPTER 17

"The money went to three different accounts. Two of them in off shore accounts and one right here. The bank is following the off shores and I'm keeping tabs on the local one. As soon as someone accesses it I'll be able to get as much information as I can off the account. Right now, we have to wait."

Pete had showed up ten minutes ago. She'd also told Shawn and Aaron that Bradley had contacted her and that he would call as soon as he got a scent. There wasn't anyone at the diner.

"Bradley said that there is a pack there. Rogues, he said. He and the others are following the scent as well as they could, but there was a car and he can't follow the scent anymore."

"So we've lost her again. I still have an hour to go before I can leave and my mate is out there somewhere with a pack of rogue wolves. Whoever this guy is, he'd better hope that Bradley gets to him before I do. I'm not going to hold my beast back when I do find him."

Shawn paced. And when he wasn't pacing he was looking at the heavily-shaded window. His body ached with the need to touch Cade. He knew she was hurt. Over the past hour he'd gotten short glimpses of her pain. Twice he'd almost gotten her to let him in. It seemed the weaker she got, the easier it was getting to be to contact her. Shawn wished he had taught her more about her kind, their kind.

"We'll get there. Bradley will be there soon if he's not already. Once we figure it out, then we'll find her. Cade has your blood, Shawn, she'll be very strong. And she's smart too."

Yeah, Shawn thought, she left the safety of the house when he'd told her to stay home. But then he really couldn't blame her for that. He'd been less than nice about it and worse yet, he'd demanded that she listen to him. He should have asked her then explained to her, given her a choice. Then, if that didn't work, fuck her until she couldn't move. He liked that idea best of all. Shawn looked up when Pic came into the room.

"We have him."

~~~

Val opened his eyes. Something was...off. Not wrong, but not quite right either. He reached out beyond the soil that he rested in and tried to find what had awakened him. At first he wasn't sure what he was feeling. As a vampire who had at one time been mated to a Lesser Faerie he had inherited her ability to feel the earth and elements of it.

Blood. He knew the taste of it, the feel of it, and this blood, fresh in his earth, he knew. Reaching further, he knew also that it was spilt in harm, harm to his. He was also able to tell that the blood had been weakened. While not yet gone he knew that this child of his was nearing her end. Carefully, so as not to scare her, he spoke to her. Spoke to her in the way of their people.

"Child, reach into the soil. Dig deep into it and ask for its help. The earth is yours and you can ask for its help. Dig deep with your toes, your fingers, dig into it and ask for help."

Val didn't think she'd answer him. He couldn't move from the earth yet as the sun was still high in the sky. He'd been entombed for decades, he knew, and he would need the earth, the soil to replenish him, to heal him until he could feed. It mattered little to him that being in this magical place he could move in the light. Val was of the old school and could not bring himself to change now and venture into the light.

"I'm too tired. I hurt. Go away. He killed her and I can't...why would he kill my mother? I just want to die too. Please, just go away."

Before he could say more Val knew that he had to choose his words carefully. His heart, long since broken, pounded in his chest, pounded for his lost love and for the child he had lost.

"The being that hit you, he killed your mother? He killed my Jasmine?" Val began making his way to the surface and a world he'd not seen in over two decades. "You will live, child of mine. Dig into the earth and seek its help. I will be there soon."

"No. He'll hurt you. He's unbalanced and he's a wolf now. You must...you can't come here. It's too dangerous. Stay away."

Val burst through the soil and shifted to his form. The eagle moved toward the tree line even as the sun warmed and nourished his skin. He had to get to her. He had to save her. Putting the most compulsion into his voice as he could, he pushed it to her.

"You'll do as I say, child of mine. Dig into the earth. The earth will help you; pull from its source. Ask for it to heal you. Do it now."

Val was in her mind because she was his daughter. He knew her name as his child Juliana, but not this adult. He moved through the sky, rushing toward her, moving between shadows and light between this world and the one she was in. He was going to save her; he was going to kill the man who dared touch what was his. Val was nearly there when he felt the others, felt the wolves as they moved as one toward her. Reaching to a higher power, looking for the master of the realm, Val found Aaron MacManus.

"I am Vladimir Michaels, vampire. My child is in mortal danger. A pack of wolves, rogues by the scent of them, move toward where she is. I ask your permission to enter your realm, to feed, and to go to her aide. I have no master now and will pledge to you if you allow me this."

"Cade MacFarland? You're her father? Her mate, Shawn MacFarland, is on his way to her. She's in trouble and has blocked him. Do you have an idea where she is?"

"She is below me in a house. The house sits beyond the road and is white. The road is called Vista View Lane. She is within the basement. A man, a newly turned wolf, is with her. He has hurt her much, her life is draining away. I wish to kill him, need to kill him, for he claims to have killed my mate as well."

"Cade's mate will be there soon. I have relayed your message to him and he wishes for you to await him before entering. I would suggest you do this. Shawn is old and powerful and he won't take it well if you don't do as he has asked."

Val bristled. He didn't want to wait. He wanted to go in and kill the wolf. But he knew that this man, MacManus, could make his life a living hell. Especially now that he knew his child was alive.

"I'll wait, my lord. That's unless it becomes life or death for my child. She will remain foremost in my heart no matter what you do to me."

"I could expect no less. I would do the same. Shawn will be there soon. He is a wolf, black and gray. He knows your scent, as we are one."

Val watched the pack move. There were seven of them, powerful yet newly turned. Val could feel their need to tear and to kill. Bloodlust was first and foremost in their minds. A movement just behind them drew his attention. Another pack, this one larger, more seasoned. Their leader was huge and in control.

Reaching to the earth Val asked that they be able to move with stealth, silent along the branches and leaves. He watched as the ground moved just in front of the leader and he stopped and looked around. Val shifted into his human form for only a minute then shifted back to the eagle. The wolf bowed and continued on his way.

Staying as the eagle Val dropped to the ground and hopped toward the house. When he was in front of it he dug his talons into the earth and asked for help. The ground moved beneath his feet, slowly at first then more as time passed. When he was sure he could move on swift, silent feet as he had done for the other pack Val shifted to his human form and moved with vampire speed to the open window. The movement of wind behind his back was his only warning. Suddenly he was pinned against the house with a massive forearm to his neck.

"You'll die if you don't give me a good enough reason right now not to kill you. I don't care if you are her dad, she's my mate. You're here without permission and I am well within my rights as second to the master. You were told to wait."

Val could feel the power surging through the man who held him. Mate, his daughter's mate. Val raised his hands in surrender and looked the older vamp in the eyes. His fangs were long and deep, his eyes, like Val's, were deep red.

"I have not moved within. The pack comes closer. I am merely in a better position in the event things go badly quickly. I need to do this one thing for her. I must be the one to save my child. You may kill me if you need after, but I need to save her when I couldn't her mother."

Val could see the indecision in his eyes. He was at least twice Val's age and more than triple the power base. Plus, Val had not fed, not fed in almost thirty years, the earth and the queen's magic keeping him alive. Just when Val was going to beg again the man let him drop to the ground.

"A pack comes. The alpha of this region wants the wolf and his pack. Only kill them if necessary and not their leader at all. Bradley is a nice wolf, but he is fucking pissed at this guy. I can sense one other with Cade. I'll...I'll grant you this so long as she is safe. The second I see one thing looking as though it may harm her you'll wish you had let me kill you now. Do I make myself clear?"

Val wanted to bow before this man. He was willing to give Val the opportunity to save his daughter. Val had no illusions about what would happen if he didn't, or if anything happened to Cade in the process. He wouldn't fail, couldn't fail. "You have my word. I will sooner let you kill me than to cause Juliana any harm. I thank you. Your name? I don't know your name."

"Shawn Alan MacFarland. Cade MacFarland is my mate. I'm guessing that you called her Juliana as a child?" Val nodded. "She doesn't know you then. Be careful not to harm what is mine, Vladimir. You do your part and we might let you hang around long enough to explain who you are to her."

When the sounds of wolves tearing into flesh, a horrific sound of screaming and breaking bones reached their ears, each vampire dematerialized and entered the house. Val went to just behind the wolf and Shawn, holding back just a few seconds, to Cade.

Wasting no time at all Val grabbed the wolf's hair and jerked him to expose his neck at the same time he became solid again. Wrapping his free arm around the wolf's waist Val sank his fangs deep into the jugular. Hot blood surged into his mouth. Drawing hard on the open vein Val swallowed the enriched essences into his starving body. Pull after pull of the wolf blood filled Val's organs, his muscles, and his skin. When the wolf struggled Val simply squeezed him tight, smiling to himself with he heard his spine snap.

Val watched as the other vamp kneeled down to
Cade. Shawn was tender as he gave her his vein,
murmuring in her ear and holding her close. There was
steel in the older vamp's eye and also love. When Shawn
turned to look at Val he had a strange smile on his face.

"You plan on coming up for air or is it your plan to
drain him? I'd say that's a good idea either way, but I
think you'd better ask the alpha first. I think he has plans
for that one. Seems they shit in his oatmeal something
fierce today."

Val had no idea what that meant, but he did stop
drinking from the man who now lay limp in his arms. He
did not bother to seal the wound. The wolf could die for
all that Val cared. He felt revitalized and strong. Stronger
than he'd felt for a very long time.

"I had no plan other than to feed and then kill him.
Will she be all right? She took quite a beating. I had her
dig into the earth to keep her safe until someone could
arrive to help her."

"I'll take care of her. You should take him to the
others. Bradley is there now and I've no doubt was
triumphant over the fools who thought to come into this
realm without so much as a text."

Val nodded and threw the wolf over his shoulder. He
took one last look at his daughter before he turned to go.
She looked like her mother so much that it hurt.

~~~

Shawn watched the man go with his burden. He'd
seen the anguish in his eyes and the need, but Shawn
wasn't ready to give her up. Not yet at any rate. He
picked Cade up and pulled her into his arms as she fed

from his wrist. Soon he would need to pull away, but for now he wanted to just hold her.

Laying her on the cot in the corner Shawn covered her with the light blanket there. Tucking it around her he kissed her forehead. She would rest now and heal. He wished that he could have killed the man who had hurt her, but Aaron had begged him to allow Vladimir to have the pleasure.

"According to Mel he's been searching for Cade since her mother's body was found. When Vladimir found his mate dead in their home and his daughter missing he'd gone into such a rage that Mel had threatened to have him put into a prison. She'd made him a deal that if he would remain true to her as her servant then she would release him from his bond mate so that he could feed and search for his daughter."

Shawn didn't think he'd want to live without Cade, but he knew that with a child involved it was all Vladimir had left to him. Kissing Cade again he left her in the basement of the house and went to search for the one who had caused it all. He knew that Aaron and Sara were on their way and that Aaron would safeguard Shawn's true love.

Shawn nearly laughed out loud when he breached the doorway and stepped out into the yard. Four men stood around a lone wolf. They looked to be bloodied and torn up. The smaller alpha in the middle was pristine and seemed to be not a little nervous. Shawn went to stand next to Bradley and Vladimir. He could feel the humor rolling off the two men.

"Problem here?" Shawn asked and then grinned wider when Bradley snorted. Val just laughed outright.

"No problem. These four seem to think that the one in the middle is someone they should be loyal to. I've given them the opportunity to join with me and...What did you say his name was again? Gabriella?" Bradley asked one of the standing men.

"You almost got it. It's Gabriel. He says that we ain't to go to you 'cause you are gonna kill us anyway." This came from the biggest of the men.

"You got that part right. I will kill you if you stand with that moron. This is the last time I make this offer. Come away from him and I'll make you a part of my pack. Provided that you behave, that is. If you stand there, say, another ten minutes, I'll sic my pack on you and kill you before you can shift back to wolf. Up to you. You're on my land, in my territory now. Pack law states that I am well within my rights to do so."

The littlest man, Bill, stepped away. When the wolf in the middle growled Bill stepped away again. He looked up at Bradley.

"I got me a family. A mate and three cubs. They come too? He said that you'd kill them just because you can. I'm not so sure that I believe him anymore."

"Smart man. Come over here and you and yours will be safe. I'm a fair man. Ask any of these men and women with me. Time is running out, gentlemen. Live or die, but hurry up and decide. My own mate is waiting for me and I tire of standing in the waning night."

Bill moved away and toward the pack. When he was close enough Bradley nodded to the other men and moved toward them. Shawn thought it was going to be bloody when suddenly the three remaining men walked toward him and Bradley, leaving their pack alpha standing alone. Bradley stopped five feet from Gabriel.

"Shift. Now." The change was immediate. Only a powerful alpha could make another shift. And Bradley was very powerful. "You have anything to say before I let this man kill you?"

Shawn was startled to realize he was talking about him. He moved to stand just beside and slightly behind Bradley. They both knew what had been done to his mate had been ordered by this man and Bradley was giving Shawn a great honor by letting him have first blood.

"You can't kill me. I'm pack, their pack. As alpha, I demand that you let—"

"Demand? You have no right to make demands here. You forfeited them when you came onto my property, when you attacked my house and my friends. You have no rights at all, Gabriella. If the woman were in any shape to demand it, I'd let her decide how you should die. Shawn, kill him."

Bradley walked away and Shawn took one step toward Gabriel. Morphing a hand into a long-clawed hook, Shawn sliced the wolf's head from his body. Even before his body dropped to the ground Shawn was walking away toward the other man, Garrett.

He lay on the ground, his back broken and his face a mass of cuts and bruises. He hadn't been able to utter a word since Val had dropped him where he now lay. Shawn wanted this man dead as well, wanted him to never be able to torment anyone or anything ever again. Only this death wasn't his. Shawn turned to Bradley. "He murdered this man's mate in cold blood, alpha. He told my mate that he killed her for the sole pleasure of a playmate when his own parents wouldn't give him one. Garrett's death belongs to Cade's father."

"He has killed more than my mate, alpha. He has killed more of your kind. He deserves to die, but not by my hand either. Melody, the queen, should have the right. He has killed over a dozen of hers over the past decade and more than he could remember before that. I have his blood, I have his memories. He should die by her hand and hers alone."

Shawn's respect for the vamp just went up. Few would allow for a crime against his mate to go unpunished and fewer still would be willing to let another take the life. Looking back at Bradley, Shawn realized that he too was impressed by Vladimir. Mel shimmered into the field almost immediately.

"Vladimir, you give me a great honor. I will take his death for all those he has killed. You, I give a boon. You will come with me when I leave. Shawn, get your mate to ground. Bradley, I hope I can depend on you to clean this mess up."

Garrett's body disappeared and a minute later so did Mel and Vladimir. Bradley looked around the clearing and snorted again. His pack began clearing the field of the other dead wolves.

"She could have done this with a wave of her hand. But no, she leaves it for us. Take Cade to your lair, feed her. Tell her that I expect some more apple dumplings soon and that I want two for myself. My bitch is whelping again and I can't seem to keep her full."

Shawn thought he didn't look the least bit upset about it and told the alpha that. Both men looked up when Cade came through the open doorway. She looked spent and weak, but by far the most beautiful thing Shawn had ever seen. He gathered her into his arms and took them home.

CHAPTER 18

Cade woke to have Shawn wrapped around her. She needed to get up, but was loath to wake him to do it. Her body ached and she needed to pee, but he was warm and hard. A perfect affirmation that she was alive. When she moved closer to the edge of the bed he pulled her back with a growl.

"Lie still. It's still a few hours till sunset and I need my rest. You should rest too. When I do get up I plan to fuck you until you can't move for at least a week."

She stilled in the bed. Images of him doing just that danced through her head and she sent them to him. His sudden stiffening made her smile and when she reached out and ran one of her fingers down his spine he growled again.

"You sound energetic to me. I don't suppose you'd like to get a start on tha—" Cade was suddenly pinned to the bed, her hands above her head and his body between her legs. She grinned up at his scowl.

"Woman! What am I going to do with you? I told you to rest. Thomas said that you would need at least twenty-four hours before you would be awake and another twenty-four before you would even contemplate wanting to have sex."

Cade ran her feet up his bare calves. Up and down until he rocked into her. Her body tightened at the thought of him fucking her. She felt her fangs lengthen and stretch in her mouth, the need to bite him imminent.

"I want you. I want to taste you and feel you inside of me. I can't wait for another minute much less another two days. Take me, Shawn. Make me forget everything but you."

Shawn's mouth gently brushed against hers. Warmth flooded her being. When he kissed her again she could feel his restraint and his need. Moving into his mind she gave him images of what she needed from him, what she wanted to do to him.

"You're killing me, love. I don't know if I can be gentle with you right now. I want you so desperately that I can't think beyond touching you. I want you so badly right now that I can't hold back."

Cade rolled Shawn to his back and sat across him. Her body covered in a t-shirt and panties was all that was between them. Lifting the shirt up and over her head she cupped her breasts and rolled her nipples. His hands dug into her hips as he pulled her forward and over his engorged cock. Her panties soaked with her juices made the slide over him easier and quicker. She rode him as she continued to squeeze her nipples.

When his hands slid up her hips, grabbed the strings of her panties, and he ripped them from her body she growled at him. His hips moved up to every one of her downward motions. When he sat up, his cock pressed hard against her clit, she grabbed his shoulders and rode him harder.

"That's it, baby, ride me. I want you to come this way so that I can feel your cum run over me. Then I'm going to eat you, suck on that hard nubbin of yours, and fuck you with my tongue. I want you to come down my throat, baby. Come and fill me with your juices."

Her body exploded. Even as she was still jerking and her body convulsing Shawn rolled her to her back and sat up. He stroked his cock as he watched her come down. When she made to lean up and take him into her mouth he pressed her back down.

"My turn. Lay back, Cade. I'm going to make you wish for that nap." He moved back on the bed, the entire time stroking his long, thick cock until she thought she'd scream at him to fuck her. When he lifted her thighs and put them over his shoulders, as he settled between her legs, Cade felt a gush of liquid pour from her body.

Shawn ran his tongue from her gate to her clit. It was all she could do not to leap up off the bed. As he inserted a finger into her she felt his breath across her folds. When he opened her soft nether lips she moaned his name. The second then the third finger moved inside of her, reaching for and finding that special spot deep within her heat. Riding his fingers now, she nearly screamed when he suckled her clit into his mouth and nipped.

"Shawn, please. Please, oh please, oh please." She couldn't think beyond what he was doing, couldn't breathe. The roaring in her ears the blood rushing through her veins made her close her eyes to try and regain some of her equilibrium. It didn't work. He was relentless.

Every time she was close, every time she could feel paradise just there, he'd pull back until she could feel her body slowing down. Then he would begin again, never really giving her relief and never touching her clitoris enough to give her release. The more she begged, the more he would make her suffer.

"I'm going to feed from you here, Cade. I'm going to bite you here on this delicious clitoris and feed from your juices and your blood. Will you come for me? Will you give me your essence and fill me?"

"Yes! Oh God, yes. Please, Shawn, I beg you give it to me. Give me relief, I beg you. Bite me and give it to me." Cade detonated. Her scream rent the air when he sank his teeth into her and when he drew hard on her she came again. Holding his head to her, she rocked up into the bite and his mouth. Over and over the waves crashed over her; more and more she rocked, and more and more he took.

When she felt his tongue slide over the bite and he sat up she nearly sobbed with it. She wasn't sure if it was because he'd stopped or because she needed more. When he moved between her legs, his cock nudging her entrance, she wrapped her legs around his hips as he slammed deep within her.

Shawn nuzzled her neck, licking his way to her beating pulse as he pulled nearly out and slammed back deep inside of her. She could feel his cock touching her, filling her even as his mouth opened over her vein. When he bit her again she screamed out and bit him too. Her fangs sank deep, his blood filled her mouth, and she came again. Sealing the tiny wounds at his shoulder Shawn roared out his release, his cum shooting deep within her, filling her with his seed and his heat. When he dropped his weight down on top of her, shifting them to the side as he rolled to his back, Cade fell into a deep, sated sleep even as she felt the covers pull over them.

~~~

Shawn woke with Cade wrapped around him. Pulling her tighter against him he marveled at how well she fit there. When she nuzzled his neck and licked his pulse he tilted his head and allowed her his vein. Her bite was gentle and he felt his cock harden with it. As she fed from him, suckling at his throat, he rubbed his hand up and down her body, feeling her move in, ready for his cock again. When his hand ran across her hip and felt the heat he stopped. Something was there.

"Baby, what's this? It's hot and it feels like a scar. I don't remember seeing it before."

Cade sealed the prick marks on his throat and stretched over him. His cock jumped in response and she smiled at him. Shawn swatted her ass and then rubbed the small injury.

"I don't know where it came from. It was there a few days ago. It looked like a faerie, but I couldn't really see it. She's gold and her wings were tight against her back. Can you look at her and see what you can see of her?"

Shawn moved her to the bed and turned so that he could see it. Even in the darkened room he could see that it was a faerie. Reaching to the bedside table he turned on a lamp. He immediately forgot about the mark he was supposed to be looking at.

Cade looked beautiful. He knew immediately that wasn't right; she'd looked beautiful before. Now she looked exquisite, radiant, like someone had painted her with a magical brush and made her more. Her eyes were bluer, her hair darker and fuller. Her skin glowed with good health and something more. Lips full from his kisses now looked plumper, more kissable, and much more delectable. He wanted her, not just for now, not just for the moment. He wanted her for all time and beyond.

Leaning in, he kissed her gently and without much pressure. Her taste filled him, urged him to take more, to mark, to taste, to fill himself on her. When he moved her to her back as he moved over her she lifted her legs and wrapped them around him. But he didn't want that. He needed to bite...bite the mark he'd only just discovered. A need like he'd never experienced had him moving down her body toward her hip.

Without saying the words she seemed to know what he needed and rolled to her side. She moved on the bed so that the mark was there for him to see, to touch, and to taste. Running his fingers over the area Cade groaned and he could swear that he could feel it too, the movement under his hand on his own skin. Licking the area, feeling the warmth spread over his tongue, Shawn looked up at Cade again.

"Yes. Please, Shawn. I need you to bite me there. Take it into your mouth and bite. Please hurry. I need it."

Licking the area again, Shawn could feel the heat, taste the warmth throughout his body. His fangs thickened in his mouth, the need to bite painful to him. Finally grazing gently over it once then again, Shawn sank his teeth into her.

Shawn heard Cade scream, not from pain but pleasure. He knew because his own body was doing the same. Wave after wave of it swept through him, over him, and through him. As the feelings moved, so did something else. He wasn't sure what it was, but a feeling of tranquility and peace moved over him. When he reached out to Cade he knew that she, too, was experiencing the same thing. Before he sealed the tiny wound and moved up her body he felt that he'd made a greater connection not just with Cade, but with everything.

Even when the burning in his own body began he wasn't surprised to see a faerie on his hip as well. His was more masculine, more defined as a male, his body different and fuller, longer even. His wings, as were the ones on Cade's faerie, were no longer tucked behind their backs, but full and open, wide and translucent. They were marked. Both wore the same golden faerie pair, their own sigils.

Exhausted from their transformation, because he had no doubt that's what had happened, Shawn pulled Cade into his arms once again and held her. Soon they were both asleep, a deeper more sated sleep than either of them had ever had.

Chapter 19

Cade made her way to the upper floors around noon the next morning. She was sore, yet her body felt somewhat lighter, more...well, more everything. Shawn was still sleeping and she had been careful not to wake him. She needed some time to herself. When she walked into the kitchen she knew that while not alone, she realized this is what she had been looking for. Duncan.

"Good morning, my lady. Shall I fix you something to break your fast? There are many things to choose from."

Out of the corner of her eye Cade saw Penny shake her head no. Cade might have laughed at the look of pure horror on the woman's face, but Cade knew that it would hurt Duncan's feelings. Taking a deep breath, she shook her head no. "Thanks, Duncan, but I'm fine. I'm a little stressed, I think. Shawn told me that I owe the alpha some apple dumplings for his help in saving me last night. Do you still have all the stuff to make them? I could do that now if you don't mind. Baking relaxes me."

It did, too. She had always been able to whip up a batch of anything and feel better because of it. The diner where she had worked had benefited from all sorts of stress related outbursts.

"Of course, my lady. All the things that you needed have been replenished. The children so loved the pancakes that you made that I have asked Miss Penny to make them for them. However, the dumplings are a mystery to us."

Cade started to mix up the crust as she thought about the last few days. In the past two weeks more things had happened to her than in an entire year. She was just rolling out the pastry when she thought about something Duncan had said.

"Duncan, why do you call me 'my lady?' Before it was just Cade. When a woman becomes a mate does she automatically become a lady? Because I have to tell you, I'm far from that title."

"I have known Master Shawn for a very long time. When I met him he was a lord. I do believe he may have been one in his previous life as well. His name then was Lord Shawn Alexander. His estate was the Mac Shriver lands. As you are now Master Shawn's mate that makes you a lady, thus her ladyship."

Cade paused in her baking. Lord and Lady MacFarland. She grinned thinking about all kinds of ways to tease Shawn with his newly discovered title.

"You will be happy to know that I've been a lord of some estate or another many times. And teasing me will get you spanked. Come back to bed. I have a need of you, my Lady Cade."

Shawn's whisper in her mind sent a shiver through her body. It was hard to get used to, this constant contact with another person. She experimented with sending him her love and she was rewarded with it returned to her.

"I'm cooking. Leave me be. How is it that I can be in the sun and you can't? I thought I was like you." Cade had actually been a little afraid to move into the bright kitchen when she'd first come to the door.

"It's probably because you are only half vampire. I think we need to talk about the sigil that we both now wear too. Is Mel there with you? I can feel her magic in the house."

"No, it's only Penny, Duncan, and me in here. I feel it too. But it's not her. It's someone that...weird. It feels like my mom. But I know that she's—" Cade turned to the man behind her and he smiled at her.

"Hello Cade. My name is Vladimir Michaels. I'm your father. I've been searching for you for a very long time."

"Cade! What happened? I'm coming up." She knew that he would, too, despite the fact that he would dissolve. "We don't dissolve. What a notion. That man, I can feel him now, he's your father. I met him at the house yesterday."

"Well, don't you think you might have mentioned this yesterday? Sheesh! A woman's father showing up is a big deal to most people. Why didn't you tell me?"

"Because, my love, I wanted to make love to you far more than I wanted to talk to you. And if I'm not mistaken, you enjoyed it too. If you need me to show you, tell them all that you are coming to aide your mate. They'll understand."

Cade blushed and her body heated when he sent her images of just want sort of aide she could give him. It was everything she could do not to start throwing off her clothes and run back downstairs to him. She turned to the room in general and knew that at least the man calling himself her father knew just what had been going on between her and Shawn. She closed off the connection when he laughed at her.

"Vampire men are such pigs. Shawn didn't tell me that you had made contact with him. I'm sorry, but I don't remember you, or my mother for that matter. I was...I guess since you were there yesterday, you know what happened to me."

"Yes. Your mate, he avenged you and me. He is a good man, I believe. As for being a pig, well, you'd know that better than I." He nodded to one of the chairs and Cade nodded back. He sat down and that was when she noticed that he had a chest with him. "The queen sent it with me. She said that it is yours through your mother. I have not seen it as of yet. She said that I would be able to answer any questions you may have about the contents."

Cade noticed that Penny and Duncan were no longer in the kitchen. She was nervous and a little scared to see what he had. That was when she felt Shawn send her warmth and love. It moved through her and made her stronger.

"I don't know what to call you. I'm sorry. I know this has got to be just as strange for you as well. The people who raised me, they never made any bones about not being my real parents and it wasn't until yesterday that I knew that Garrett had killed them. Shawn told me that the queen took him away. Do you know what happened to him?"

"Garrett is dead. The queen decided that he should be killed in the manner that he was most familiar with and the way of the lives he took. He was a cruel and heartless man. His victims were tortured in ways that are beyond what nightmares are made of. Faeries can be very...how should I say...vicious when they need be. He suffered greatly for his crimes."

Cade shuddered. She wasn't sure how a faerie could be considered vicious, but the tone that Vladimir used gave her no doubt that Garrett did suffer. She looked down at the chest. She wasn't entirely sure what to do about it either. Her father seemed to read her mind.

"We can leave it for another time. I would like to ask you about your mark. I know that you and your mate have merged. It is a magic like no other. You, especially, will notice the difference. Your magic will be stronger. You will be able to summon the earth and the elements to you."

"I don't have any magic. I mean, I didn't before we...that's before Shawn and I...we... I don't have any magic." Cade could feel herself blush again. She knew that magic was what gave her the ability to bite Shawn, but she was sure there was nothing else. A little overwhelmed, she got up to finish the dumplings.

"You do have it, child. You have used it, too, twice since I have entered this room. You have summoned the flour to you and you have the oven turned on to use. You have a great deal of magic, mine as well as your mother's. She was a powerful Lesser Faerie. The Queen was quite proud of her."

Cade looked at the flour. Had she? She didn't know. She had caught herself doing it when she was younger and had been very careful since. Garrett would hurt her...he was dead and could no longer hurt her, she thought. Maybe that's why she was using it more, because she felt safer.

"What is a Lesser Faerie? I mean, I've heard the term and I do have a mark. It's a faerie on my hip. I don't understand what it means to me. Or to Shawn for that matter."

Mel shimmered in the room. Cade tried not to be a little uneasy around the being, but she made Cade feel things she'd never felt before. Subservient came to mind.

"Oh, for heaven's sake. Your mother said that same thing to me a hundred times. I've never felt that she was subservient to me. She was my friend, as I would like for you to be." Mel turned to Vladimir. "You're right. She does look like her mother. She was very beautiful and I have felt her loss for a great many years."

Cade held onto the counter. The room swam dizzily around her. She felt Shawn moving and she didn't try to stop him. Something was wrong. Something was very wrong.

"Someone is coming. Someone is coming here now. I can feel their hatred and violence. They want...they want me. I can't ..."

"Cade, look at me. Cade! Look at me, tell me what you feel. Who is coming?" Shawn was holding her. She vaguely realized he was standing in the kitchen with her.

"It's a man. He is angry with...with you. He thinks you are the cause of his downfall. That the Council is after him because of what you did. I don't understand. What does that have to do with anything?"

"It's my master. I turned him in to the Council because he was killing humans. I have to get you to safety." She felt his terror as if it were her own. He was afraid for her. "Mel, can she stay with you? I can't have her—"

"I'm not going anywhere. You said we were mates. I go where you go. If you even try that mind thingy on me I'll personally make it so you can't walk for the rest of your long life."

"He'll hurt you to get to me. You have to understand that he's powerful and that I can't lose you. You have to obey me on this, Cade. I'm not kidding."

"Obey you? Are you for real? I obey no one, fang face. I will listen to suggestions, reasonable ones anyway, but you won't tell me what to do and expect me to hop to it. If you do, it's going to be a very long eternity for you." Cade flushed when she heard her father laugh. She turned on him in a heartbeat. Embarrassed or not she didn't think it was a laughing matter. "Listen here, bucko. You think this is funny? Then you can kiss any father-daughter dances goodbye. I am not going anywhere. Now, what's the plan?"

"I would in no way laugh at you, my dear. I was just thinking how very much like your mother you are. Shawn, you might as well give it a rest. She will wear you down. I had it happen to me many times in the centuries I lived with her mother."

"I cannot take her to my kingdom anyway," Mel said. "I am bound by your laws of the challenge. If you fail to win, Cade is his to do with what he pleases. I can't stop him, nor can I condemn him, not about that. You will have to face Ferris with Cade at your side or not."

Before Cade could form an answer or even begin to wonder about her father spending centuries with her mother both Sara and Aaron came into the room. It seemed they too could feel the creature making his way toward them. Cade was afraid. Not for herself, but for those around her. She looked up at Shawn and knew that he was as well. Cade was just going to suggest that they leave now before he hurt any of them when Aaron spoke up.

"You have a choice, Shawn and Cade. Challenge him and kill him, or run. If you run you'll never be a master. If you stay you chance losing Cade. But I know that you can beat him. He is a young vamp who has risen to what he is by terror and murder. You are strong, Shawn. Your age and your newly acquired magic gives you an advantage over others and he wouldn't be expecting it."

"What do you mean by challenge him? You mean fight him? To the death? I don't think so. I may be new to this whole mate thing, but there is no way you are going to challenge some guy because he's pissed off. Hello? It's been my experience that pissed off men tend to fight dirty." Cade looked around the room. They all avoided looking back except the queen.

"It would do him no good to run. Ferris will come and destroy what he leaves behind. Cade, with your added magic, Shawn will win. You must have faith in him."

Cade looked at Sara. Realization dawned on her. They were hoping for Shawn to fight this guy. And, for whatever reason, thought that she would aide him in some way when he did. And if she failed him they would both die.

"He's here. I can feel him now. He is outside. Cade, stay inside until I talk with him. Maybe I can convince him that you aren't a part of this. Please listen to me, you have to stay inside."

When Shawn moved toward the door Cade was too shocked to follow. Her heart was thundering in her chest and the roaring in her head was making thought nearly impossible. Shawn was going to die and it would be her fault. She looked at the two women who had stayed with her. Sara looked worried and Mel looked...looked pleased. There was something so eerie about her smile that Cade closed her eyes against it.

Cade only had one choice. And she moved toward the door before either of them could stop her. She knew what she had to do.

The four men, Aaron, Shawn Vladimir and Ferris, stood in the yard just behind the house. Ferris was asking Shawn how he could have done such a thing to him. Cade could feel his anger, not at Shawn and what he'd done, but that he'd been caught and was now having to stand trial for it. He thought killing Shawn would be a way to stop the trial. Then she could feel him, she knew who he was.

"I thought we were friends, Shawn. I can't believe that you'd turn me in without asking me if this was true. You've no proof, that's what the Council said, you've no proof."

"I do, though, don't I? You took the money, or at least you made me take it. You're the guy who ordered me to steal the money from all those people," Cade interrupted.

"I don't know what the hell you're talking about. What money? This girl is insane. She should be locked up."

Ferris started to back away from Cade. She walked to him until she felt a hand on her arm. She didn't even turn to look at Shawn, but continued talking to Ferris. "I remember you from when you came to the office. You told Gabriel that if I didn't do as you said he was to make me understand that you were the boss. He did. He beat me so badly that I spent seven days in intensive care."

"Cade, you sure this is the man? Is he the one who Gabriel was working for? You sure about this?"

"Yes, Mr. MacManus, I'm sure. He hit me. And when he did I grabbed onto his shirt and tore it. He has a tattoo on his left breast. It's a heart with a knife through it."

"She's nuts. Vamps can't tat, you know that as well as anyone. Hell, all it does is make us a little sore for an hour then it's gone. I tried it once a long time ago. I've never seen this girl in my life."

"Then perhaps you won't mind if we have a look at your chest. It won't take a minute and then you can finish your business with me. I, for one, have never seen your chest, might be a moving experience." Shawn moved to stand in front of Cade. She tried getting around him, but he'd have none of it.

"I don't know where you get off talking to me that way, Shawn. I'm your master. You should have more respect for me than that."

Cade finally got around Shawn and moved two steps toward Ferris. Her intent was to tear his shirt from his body. But that's not what happened. Just as she moved in front of Shawn Ferris issued his demand with a raised hand.

"I challenge you. I challenge you to the death."

CHAPTER 20

"Mother fuck. I told you to stay in the house. I begged you to. But you couldn't, could you? You just had to come out and challenge him. Why didn't you just tell me through our link what you suspected?"

Shawn had been ranting for the past ten minutes. Cade sat in the kitchen chair and didn't say a word. Not a word to him or anyone else in the room. He wasn't sure why, but that bothered him a great deal.

"Cade, sweetheart, you need to listen to me. You can't win against this man. He's not very old, but he knows how to—"

"So I was supposed to support you and you don't have to support me? That doesn't sound very good, does it? Or is it because I'm just a Lesser Faerie and not a two-thousand-year-old vampire who lives off of other people's blood?"

"That's not what I meant. He has more experience. He knows how to fight and he won't play by any rules. It's to the death. Do you understand what that means?"

When she looked up at him Shawn's heart clenched. He'd hurt her. Not physically, but he'd hurt her all the same.

"Yes. I'm well aware of what death means. If you don't mind, I need to take a short nap. I want you to stay away from me for a little while."

Cade left the kitchen. When Shawn made to follow her Vladimir stopped him. He looked at her father and started to snarl at him to mind his own business when he realized the man was smiling.

"She'll win this challenge. There isn't any way for her not to. I put her mother's chest in her room. Cade will look and realize what she has, what she is. You will be fine. What I would do if I were you is wonder how you are going to make her happy."

"He's going to kill her. I can't...even without the need of her blood I couldn't live without her. She is my life, can't you understand that?"

As soon as the words were out of his mouth Shawn regretted them. Of course Vladimir would know. His own mate had been taken from him along with Cade. He started to tell the vampire that when Vladimir started talking.

"I met Cade's mother just before I turned. I'm a pure blood so my change was different from yours. At thirty-five I went through the transformation and became what you see today. I'd had years of training preparing me for what I'd be, what I'd need to do to survive, and how I was to survive. Most of it is imprinted into us before birth, but a lot is from the experience of those around us."

Shawn didn't know what this had to do with what Cade had done, but he didn't interrupt. He wanted to know the man who had lived for nearly three decades looking for a child he didn't know had lived or not.

"Jasmine was centuries older than me. When I met her she had already lived several of my lifetimes and yours as well. But she was mine. I knew it as soon as I touched her." Vladimir stood up and began pacing. Shawn had seen Cade do the same thing. He wondered if it was hereditary to want to pace. "When we mated and bonded in the way of our kind, vampires, I knew there was something more, something that Jasmine needed. It was nearly a century before she told me that I had not bonded with her. She said to share her sigil with a mate was something few Lesser Fairies did."

"Why?" Shawn asked just as Mel shimmered in the room and sat quietly next to him. She had the most serene look on her face. Vladimir didn't seem to notice either interruption.

"Her mark was a faerie, a golden faerie. She told me that I would become beyond myself when I took the sigil into me. I wasn't sure what she meant, but I was willing to do most anything for her. She was so..." Vladimir's voice caught so Shawn waited. "She was so excited to share this part of her. Everything she was, everything she had done, experienced, lived, said, smelled, or touched became mine. I knew all that she knew, including her magic."

"That's what makes Lesser Fairies what they are. It isn't that they are diminutive, it's because the next generation needs to know less and less because of what they pass on to each other. They are the most brilliant beings ever created. I need them more than I need my next breath. Jasmine was my friend," Mel told him. "No, not just my friend, but the sister of my heart. I would do anything for her, and her for me."

"That's why you haven't died. You haven't died because of the friendship between Jasmine and Mel. She let you live because of the connection." Shawn had wondered how Vladimir had lived without his mate. And now he knew.

"Yes. And Mel is Cade's godmother." Shawn sat back in the chair.

He could understand it now. It wasn't just a father's love for his child; it was a woman who had lost her friend and a child too. They both had suffered great loss, each of them needing Cade.

"When a being is killed like Jasmine was her magic goes to the one who killed her. In this case, Garrett. I'm not sure he ever understood what was making him do most of the things he'd do magically, but for the most part he was totally unaware of the magic in his body. So when he was killed the magic was supposed to go to his killer and so on and so forth. In this case, I was the killer. Jasmine's magic came back to me. And now I have given it back to her daughter."

Shawn knew he was supposed to be getting something. Something important, as a matter of fact, but he wasn't. Magic transferred from killer to killer. It seemed slightly macabre, but he'd seen worse things over his lifetime. Just as he started to ask he felt Cade. Power moved through her and into him. Surges and surges of energy and magic. His body stiffened with it, his head spun. When he reached for something, anything,

Mel grabbed his hand and started talking. He couldn't understand her. Cade, he had to get to Cade.

"I'm fine. Please, I'm fine. I can feel you. Listen to me, I'm fine." Her voice sounded far away, yet inside of him.

"What is that? What's happening?" Shawn could feel something burning through her and into him. His heart pounded hard in his chest at first then slowed to a normal rate. Energy flowed through them.

"I'm learning. My mother's things, there was a necklace, a moonstone I think. I put it on, felt compelled to put it on, and everything, and I mean everything, came rushing into me. She really was very beautiful. And she loved my father so much."

Shawn looked at first Mel then at Vladimir. He had to concentrate hard on what they were saying. He could barely make sense of anything for a few minutes.

"...to make it work. Are you listening to me? Shawn! Pay attention. Cade will need to go through her mother's things and see what she was left." Mel turned to Vladimir. "I don't think he's paying attention. I think he's in la-la land or something."

"I hear you. And she already has. She said there was a necklace. She thinks it's a moonstone. Cade said she felt compelled to put it on." Shawn turned to Vladimir. "I don't suppose you'd know anything about that, would you?"

Vladimir looked guilty and Shawn knew that he'd put the compulsion on the necklace. He was about to comment when he felt Cade moving toward them. Laughter and warmth surrounded him.

"I'll take care of my father. And I knew that something was off about it as soon as I touched it. Shawn, will you forgive me for this? I only meant to protect you. I never meant for this to happen."

"I know that, love. And I want to protect you as well. I can feel what you've learned. You are so powerful. Maybe more so than me."

"Never that. You hold my love. That makes you supreme in my book." She walked through the door and his breath caught.

Cade had changed. Everything about her was more. He couldn't really say what it was, but he couldn't take his eyes off of her. She glowed with health and well being; her body moved with more grace and confidence. Even her eyes seemed to hold more beauty, and vastly more strength.

"No, love. You are more powerful."

~~~

Cade grinned at him. She did feel different. And her head was buzzing with information. Her body felt heavier, stronger, and more agile. She felt as if she could fly. And shifting through the information in her head she realized that she could. There was so much, everything her mother had ever been, everything she'd ever done, and everything she'd ever felt was there for her to touch and to remember. And not just her and her mother, but generations of her family. Their knowledge and understanding of what they were, and what they could do.

"I see you found your heritage. You are a full Lesser Faerie, Cade, and a vampire. Both your parents have given you all that they are and you will pass it on to your daughter as well." Mel stood and embraced Cade. "Welcome to my kingdom. I expect great things from you from now on."

"My daughter. You look so much like your mother right now. I can't believe how much. I'm very proud of you, my girl. If you have any questions please feel free to voice them. I plan to spend every waking moment getting to know you."

Cade laughed when Shawn growled. She reached out and ran her hand along his shoulders. She could feel his strength and his love. Moving in closer, not able to help herself, she burrowed her face in his neck. Another growl, this one definitely more intimate, sent shivers down her spine and she moved back before she embarrassed them both.

"There are things you need to know about tonight. Rules of engagement. Aaron is coming and he will help explain what will happen. You must do this, Cade."

Aaron walked in the room and kissed Cade on the cheek and laughed at Shawn. He really wasn't happy about people, men especially, touching her. She wondered what it was and made a mental note to ask Sara about it.

"There are different levels of what will happen. The first is that you meet in a neutral place. Bradley has offered his land for that use. You will each have a second and that person alone will be on the field with you. This person will offer you nothing more than support. No blood can be exchanged and no magic on the second's part. In the case of you two, as a mated pair, Shawn's help will come to you naturally. The second is the drawing of first blood." Aaron bared his forearm for her.

There was a long scar there. "When I fought Carl for this realm, he drew blood and that scar will never leave me. The same will happen to you and Ferris. It's a mark of honor. If I wasn't able to show you this, I'd be the one who lost."

"If he drew first blood then why are you here? I'm sorry, that sounded crass. I mean if he drew your blood, why did you win?"

"No problem. I didn't say he drew first blood, I said he drew blood. You are the one challenged so you will go first. If you draw blood with your first strike then you will get to try and draw it again. This is how it works, you will keep getting to draw his blood until you don't. Once you fail that he gets his turn until he doesn't. If neither of you manage to draw blood then it becomes a free for all and the rules of engagement are no longer used. It's a fight to the death."

"What happens if he doesn't play by the rules? I mean, he isn't exactly a nice guy. I want to know if something happens to keep him from killing me." Cade held onto Shawn's hand. She wasn't going to leave him, not now.

"You quit the field. If at any time he moves out of turn or he cheats—which he will undoubtedly do, then you simply say that you will 'quit the field.' It's important that you word it that way. If you simply leave or say 'fuck you,' as you are prone to do, then he will win."

"And he wins." Cade didn't have to ask what his winning would be. He would destroy not only her, but Shawn and anyone else he might feel who had been a part of his downfall, including Aaron.

They talked for another hour and when the sun was at its peak, Shawn took Cade to his lair. She needed him in the worst way. And he seemed to know that. As soon as they entered the room and he locked the door she started to back toward the bed.

"I want to feel you inside of me. Deep, hard, and fast. Do you think you can help me with that?" Cade began unbuttoning her shirt as she went.

"Yes. Cade, you'd better hurry faster than that or those clothes aren't going to make it. If I have to I'm going to rip them from you, and I won't be gentle about it."

Cade felt her body respond to his words. Her pussy gushed with cream and her nipples hardened under the shirt. Shawn's eyes had turned a deep red and she could just make out the tips of his fangs at his lips. Taking both sides of the shirt she ripped it from her body. His growl made her start to pant.

"Strip off the rest. Now. I want to see you, all of you." Shawn's voice was deep, almost dark with need. It made her want to please him. Stripping down to her panties she watched as he came toward her.

"You have made me hurt with need today. You should be spanked. But I know that if I touch you right now I may enter you and come at the same time."

Cade's body tightened. "Okay" was all she could say. As soon as he touched her she knew that she wouldn't last either. And when he dropped down in front of her and ripped her panties from her she felt her knees wobble.

Shawn's mouth was hot, not just hot but white hot, as he licked her clitoris. Cade grabbed a handful of his hair and held onto him tight. When she felt his hand move to between her thighs she opened her stance for him and growled when he inserted his fingers deep into her. Over and over he fucked her this way and every time she got close to releasing the pent-up need he would move back and kiss her thigh.

"Please, Shawn. I need you inside of me. Right now." Her body ached and she nearly screamed when he nipped at her clit. Looking down at him she nodded to him, need a living, breathing thing in them both.

When Shawn sank his fangs into her thigh she came apart over him. Her climax was all-consuming and earth-moving. And as her body was still tumbling down he sealed the tiny wounds and stood. At some point he had unleashed his cock and it was straining toward her. With a quick turn and a shove Cade found herself lying on her stomach and Shawn behind her.

Grabbing her hips and pulling her back, he entered her hard. Her body needing him clutched tightly around him and she could feel his breath on her shoulder. His teeth scraping along her shoulder and neck had her growling back at him. He leaned down and whispered in her ear. "My little fighter, I'm not going to last. I'm going to bite you and when you come I want you to give me your throat. I want to taste your hot blood while you come."

As soon as his words left his mouth he sat up, pulled his cock out of her to his tip, and then slammed back into her. If he continued like this she wasn't going to last either. And she didn't. When he thrust into her the third time she screamed out his name, and when he leaned down and bit her shoulder she came again, sobbing his name until she was hoarse from it. Lifting her up so that she sat on his lap he tilted her head back and licked the pounding pulse. His fangs sinking deep into her had her come again. Stars burst behind her eyelids and the room became a brilliant light just before she fell into sated darkness.

CHAPTER 21

At sunset that evening Cade and Ferris met in the open field of the pack grounds. Bradley offered the area because it was secluded and it was open enough so that the combatants would have room to fight. No one was sure what was going to happen, but neither Cade nor Shawn seemed upset about it. Both had taken on a very calm and surreal approach to what was coming.

Cade approached the field to the north and Ferris to the south. Mel had assured everyone that she would make sure that Ferris was alone. She told them that he was bragging how he was getting a two-for-one deal in that he'd get Cade and Shawn when Cade lost. Pete had shown up about mid-day. She had tracked down where the money had gone.

"Ferris is the last man. The other three accounts were one to each man, Gabriel and Garrett and now this man. It seems that Ferris is buying up property all over the world and accumulated a mass fortune. The money moves in and out quickly so there isn't much of a paper trail, but there is another account, one that Cade set up and used that belongs to Ferris. He keeps his realm monies in it."

"So he did take the money. Lying bastard. So we can call this off. Everybody can go home happy and Cade doesn't have to fight him." Aaron looked so hopeful that Cade hated to burst his bubble.

"Yes, I do. According to Mel if I don't fight him he wins. He will own Shawn and me until either he dies or we do. And I'm ready. I want this over with."

Neither Cade nor Shawn had told anyone about the magic. They had decided that the less people who knew, the safer everyone would be. That was why she was standing in an open field waiting for the signal to begin.

Cade had first shot, so to speak. Cade hoped that he wouldn't get his chance. So long as she continued to draw blood she could keep hurting him. If neither of them were able to draw blood then all bets were off and they went after each other in a mortal showdown. Cade wasn't sure she could beat him that way so she and Shawn would keep him bleeding.

"Well, girly, are you ready to die? I certainly hope you've made your funeral arrangements and notified your next of kin. I'm going to enjoy killing you."

Cade kicked off her shoes and dug her feet into the cold ground. She could feel it begin to warm beneath her. As soon as Mel said "time" Cade reached into the soil and asked for its help.

The ground began to tremble and shake. Not much at first, but enough to make Ferris look around. When the ground heaved him over onto his back he jumped up with a small cut in his hand. It was first blood.

"No! That's not fair. You can't count the ground moving as her. She didn't do it. There was a tremor and I fell, that's not first blood." Ferris started toward Mel and drew up short when Aaron stepped in front of her.

"Really? Did I call 'time?' Are you bleeding? Then it's first blood. Cade, go again. And you, Ferris, you move toward me again and it will be a forfeit. Stay where you are until I say differently."

When Cade raised her hand a leaf sliced open his cheek. It wasn't much, but again, it was first blood. Cade was simply trying to get used to what she had to work with. Her knowledge of her powers were massive, but knowing how to use something because someone told you and knowing because you've used it were two different things altogether. Mel called Cade winner again.

Taking a deep breath she blew it toward the man across the field from her. She had simply been exhaling. Ferris dropped to the ground as if she'd shot at him. She burst out laughing before she could snap her mouth closed.

"You think this is funny, bitch. I'll show you funny. See how funny you think this is, you stupid cunt."

The magic came at her hard. He had thrown a bolt of lightning at her and if she hadn't been so one with the earth she may have fallen over. As it was she only took a step back; the bolt fell to the ground without so much as singeing her shirt. She laughed out loud again. "You lose, mother fucker. By right of vampire law I claim all that you have. You cheated. I win. I quit the field."

A stirring in the air was all the warning she had. She wasn't sure what was happening, but turned and held up her hands at the same time. Energy shot from her fingers and bolted across the distance in a heartbeat. Ferris, coming at her full tilt, was caught in it. His body exploded. One minute he was there and then next, blood and small fragments of him were strewn across the field.

No one moved, no one said a word as the ground absorbed the carnage. Cade, using a great deal of what was left of her depleted energy, turned back toward Shawn and took two steps before she crumpled to the ground. Her body gave up as she slid into darkness, the moonstone around her neck pulsing slightly.

~~~

Shawn looked around the house they had inherited. It was nothing short of a mansion like Aaron's had been, but lacked warmth and love. He hoped that he and Cade would soon change that. His servant for centuries, Mason, stood in the kitchen with Cade and surveyed the room. Shawn would have laughed if he wasn't afraid the man would quit.

"You aren't listening to me, Mason. I don't want you to learn to cook. I need you for other things in a house this big. I want you to hire someone to cook for me. You will be much too busy trying to keep up with me and the rest of the household. You are much more important to me right now than Shawn is."

Mason turned to look at him and had the most pained expression on his face. Like Shawn, the poor man wanted more than anything to please the young faerie, but neither of them had been in a household that required food for centuries. Much less one that would require a household.

"She's right, old man. If it wasn't for the sex I think she'd throw me out over you in a second. Just give in, I usually do. It's easier in the end and she'll wear you down anyway. Put an ad in the paper for a cook, Cade will do the interviewing for you, and all you'll need to do is make sure that there is someone to help out."

"But, sire, this is all so...all so different. I'm not sure what to make of all of this. You are and have always been my master and I am proud to serve you, but the young miss, she is...I think that you should help me with this. You should have to...I believe you said 'deal' with her for a bit."

Shawn flushed. He had said that when Mason had first come to the mansion and now with Cade looking at him as if he was in deep trouble he wished that Mason had kept that little bit of information to himself. Cade looked to be not at all happy with him.

"I'm not at all happy with you bucko. You're going to pay for this, you know. I think I'll invite my dad to stay for a few years. That should curb your spouting off at the mouth whenever you want. I think maybe I'll put him in the—"

Shawn picked Cade up and threw her over his shoulder. He was turning to leave the kitchen when he glanced over at Mason. He had the most grateful look on his face. Shawn reached up and swatted Cade on the ass as he moved. When she bit him in his backside, he hit her harder. Living with her was never going to be dull, he knew that.

"Shawn, put me down. You don't want to hurt the baby, do you?"

He stopped dead in his tracks. He didn't think he'd heard her right. "Cade?" Forming the next words became impossible, so he waited. When he didn't think she'd answer him, she finally did.

"Pete told me this morning. She said that I was going to have a child and that you and I needed to name the babe after her. I never did figure out why she thought so, but there you have it. I have a...what are you doing?"

Shawn laid her on the sofa as gently as he could. He had hit her. Not hard really, but he had. When he splayed his hand over her flat belly he looked up at her. "Do you think I was too rough? I...shit, Cade, you should have told me when you first found out. I spanked you and you let me. What if I had...what the hell are you laughing at? This isn't funny."

"Yes, it is. You should see your face. You look like I've just told you that you were going to die. It's just a baby, silly. Women have been doing it a lot longer than even you've been around. I'm not going to break. I'm perfectly fine."

"I don't care how many women have had one before you. This is my first one. You will take it easy from now on. And no more sex. I mean it, Cade. No more seducing me. And when we do have sex it will be gently and I'll be...stop laughing at me, damn it."

Every time he thought she was finished laughing she'd take one look at him and start all over. He wasn't amused. Shutting her up seemed a good idea and he pulled her to him—gently—and kissed her. The kiss deepened before he knew it and she was lying back on the sofa, her legs wrapped tightly around him.

"What am I going to do with you, woman? You make me nuttier than a fruit cake one second and nearly out of my mind with need the next. I love you so very much."

"And I you. Just love me, Shawn. That's all I want. Just for you to love me."

Shawn knew he would. He had no choice in the matter. She owned his heart anyway.

ABOUT THE AUTHOR

Hello! My name is Kathi Barton and I'm an author. I have been married to my very best friend Sonny for at times seems several lifetimes – in a good way, honey. And together we have three wonderful children and then the ones we brought into the world - Paul and Dale Barton, Jason and Wendy Barton and Danielle and Ben Conklin. They have given us seven of the greatest treasures on Earth. They don't live at home seven days a week! No, seriously, seven grandchildren – Gavin, Spring, Ben, Trinity, Sarah, Kelly and Kian.

www.ingramcontent.com/pod-product-compliance
Lightning Source LLC
Chambersburg PA
CBHW020611180626
46810CB00007B/2725